Praise for STARS LIKE FIRE

"Honestly, might be better than book 1!
This book continues the story of Téa, while also giving us two more adventures to follow. All three of these stories weave together to create a community that you root for and an environment where all the pieces are constantly moving, leaving you absolutely unable to put this book down. I felt like this author definitely grew through book one and was able to pour more heart and character development into this story and I am here for it! The story is beautiful and, as with book one, the message of hope and strength shines through.
Can't wait for the next installment!" ~Mae, Goodreads Review

"Marissa has done it again! She continues her unique story where love is an overarching theme. It's raw, it's emotional, and she tugs on our heartstrings even more. She's keeping me guessing and I can't wait to see how this story resolves!" ~Amber Crook, Goodreads Review

"This one had me in my feels so much! Continuing this series is wonderful and I would rate this over 5 stars because it's that good and so entertaining!" ~TheEnrichmentOfFiction, Goodreads Review

"A fantastic continuation of the first book! Marissa Lupes writing is incredible. The story is so good that I couldn't put it down." ~Amanda Bartley, Goodreads Review

Also By Marissa Lupe

Book One:
STARS LIKE ACID
Book Two:
STARS LIKE FIRE

The Bone Inventory

Marissa Lupe

Howlite Publishing LLC

Howlite Publishing LLC
Meeker, CO
United States
marissalupe.com
The Bone Inventory

First Edition, 2024
This is a work of fiction. Names, characters, business, events, and incidents are the products of the author's imagination. Any resemblance to actual persons, living or dead, or actual events is purely coincidental.
eBook ISBN: 978-1-960824-06-6

Paperback ISBN: 978-1-960824-07-3

Hardback ISBN: 978-1-960824-08-0

Library of Congress Control Number: 2024911104

Fiction/Science Fiction/General

Formatting interior book design and cover art by

Howlite Publishing LLC

To all those thinking alien abduction might not be that bad… same.
And for those still searching for their cosmic love, trust your instincts.

Note to readers...

The Bone Inventory is a standalone novel that doubles as a prequel to the STARS LIKE ACID series. You do not have to read the series in order to read this book.

This novel includes difficult subject matter including alien abduction, medical experimentation, torture, thoughts of suicide, murder, death, foul language, lots of foul language, genocide, and witch persecution.

Contents

1. Six Underground 1
2. Cumbersome 8
3. Need A Favor 17
4. Cosmic Love 27
5. The Pot 37
6. Dreams 44
7. Nothing Else Matters 47
8. Slide 56
9. Teardrop 66
10. It's Been Awhile 75
11. Bad Guy 88
12. Unwell 96
13. Wonderwall 104

14. To Be Alone With You 116

15. Around The Sun 125

16. I Am Everything 133

17. Unwanted 145

18. Save Yourself 157

19. End Of The Old Times 168

20. Everything You Want 174

21. The Mission 186

22. Savin' Me 191

23. A Storm Is Going To Come 206

24. Jumper 211

25. The Kids Aren't Alright 220

26. Epilogue 231

Stay Tuned... 236

About the Author 237

Chapter One

Six Underground

The moon did not sing tonight. It shone fiercely, piercing his eyes against the thick darkness of night. He stumbled again as he made his way through the deteriorating and overgrown graveyard. The crumbling stone and weeds that seemed to want to devour him were like a living breathing creature; ready and waiting to pull him past this side of the dirt to the place where the dead lived.

A shiver ran down his spine as he continued along what he thought was the path. Cold mist floated in slowly at first, covering his sneakers, until finally the heavy fog had risen to his knees, creating soft waves of cloud with every step. His breathing increased and ears strained. It was too quiet.

He froze, listening to the sound of his own beating heart. Before him, there came a silhouette of a tall slowly moving figure.

What was it his learner had told him about this place? Be bigger, be louder than the beasts. Swallowing his fear, he spread his shoulders puffing his chest out and shouted the first thing that came to mind.

"What the fuck!" He shouted into the shadows.

But the figure didn't even twitch as it continued to move toward him. He swallowed hard and tried to think of what a bear might sound like.

"Rar, RAR RAR RAR!" He growled as best he could, but the dark shadow kept crawling toward him.

The shape began to clear, and he was finally able to make out the shape of a face with sparkling blue eyes, crinkled at the corner from holding back laughter.

He took a deep breath. "What in the actual fuckity of fucketry is this fucking bullshit!" He shouted.

His oldest friend stood before him and could no longer hold back. His laughs bellowed out, echoing into the night.

His friend continued to laugh at him as he ground his teeth and crossed his arms. He ignored the laughter and said. "This place gives me the creeps. These *humans* bury their dead bodies, like *keepsakes.*" He cringed. "Give me the automated inventory rows any day of the week over this. You know-"

He was about to say his friends true name, but his friend held up a hand. "Stop, you know that's not my name on this planet, *Brad.*"

Brad rolled his eyes. "I hate these stupid names, *Spencer*." He whispered under his breath. "Fucking goodie two-shoes." He held out his arms and spun in a half circle like he was trying to look at his own ass. "And I hate these bodies, their so.. so.. I don't know, *bulbous*."

Spencer looked down at his own body. "They aren't exactly flattering, are they?" He lifted his shirt and stared at the six ropes of solid muscle. "So bland, typically only one color per body. Too bad more humans don't have Vitiligo, such a beautiful coloring comes with it. What a shame." He put his shirt back down and shook his head. "But that's beside the point. We have a role to play, data to collect. These were deemed to be the most likely forms able to gather the intel we need. Young white attractive adult males. People tend to trust them, listen to them, no matter how many red flags they may have. A convenient body choice."

Brad huffed and rolled his eyes. "Whatever." He said.

Spencer started to walk away back down the path. He spoke over his shoulder to Brad. "And watch your language, too many crude words can be off-putting, especially to the females."

Brad groaned and dragged his feet as he followed Spencer. "But they're the most colorful! They're so sharp and fun to say."

Spencer chuckled. "You do have a point." He paused. "Okay, one more time, and then lock it up, *Brad*."

Brad stopped and smiled wide, flashing a perfect row a brilliant white teeth. "I hate your stupid fucking face." He said to Spencer. Then he dropped his arms behind him and shouted to the sky. "Fuck this place!"

Spencer shot him a playful grin. "Are you done now?"

"Yeah, I'm done." His momentarily forgotten unease came flooding back with the oppressive silence of the night. The dead bodies under the Earthen floor were like imaginary tentacles rising up to pull him under. "Can we get out of here now? Please?"

"I wish." Spencer wiggled as though he were shaking off a hoard of bugs. "This place gives me the heebie jeebies. But we haven't found what we're looking for yet."

"It should be about here." Brad swayed his arms out in front of him trying to clear away the rolling moist fog, staring at one headstone, and then the next. They had been searching for so long that his back hurt from being bent over and his eyes were tired from the strain, when finally, Spencer shouted in the distance.

"Here! I found her!"

Brad hurried over to where Spencer waited and halted to a stop by his side. In front of them stood a large statue of an angel illuminated from the moonlight. She had a chunk of one wing missing and her grey stone face was mostly sanded down from the ravages of time, she had only one eye left.

Spencer pointed to a bronze plate below her feet, the edges corroded green by nature.

Here lies Elizabet
The best among us, taken too soon.
1826-1854

Spencer gestured to the ground. "The honor is all yours, friend."

Brad's stomach turned at the thought of the worms just below his feet, no doubt devouring whatever organic matter they could and a sour taste at the back of his throat brought an abundance of saliva to his mouth. He pushed the feeling aside and kneeled down, placed a fist flat against the dirt, pulled back, and slammed his knuckles through the ground causing a thunderous explosion of flying debris. Where there was solid ground moments before, there was now a crater six feet down. Brad hopped and landed lightly on the balls of his feet. He easily ripped away the heavy slab to Elizabet's coffin, the sound of stone smashing somewhere above him drifted to where he crouched. He sifted around until he found what he was looking for. The Stapes bone. The smallest bone in the human body residing in the middle ear, responsible for transmitting sound waves from the air outside to the fluid-filled labyrinth of the human brain.

Brad held it on the tip of his finger, then dropped it down into the center of his palm. He took one last look before tilting his head back and opening his jaw wide, it stretched unnaturally so, and he swallowed the fragment whole. He clamped his jaw shut then stood and shook off a layer of dust. With the strength and grace of a gazelle, Brad jumped out of the crater in one leap to where Spencer waited for him.

"It's done." Brad said.

"Was it her?" Spencer asked.

Brad rolled his tongue around his teeth before answering. "Yes." Brad replied.

"Good. Now let's get out of here, shall we?"

"Yes, please!" Brad said dramatically.

Brad's mind was instantaneously overwhelmed with memories of Elizbet's life as they walked. Soon, her mind would be more present than his. Until every flash of life she had lived was done flowing through Brad's consciousness, she would be a part of him. She was powerful, it would take at least two sunrises before he would have clarity back.

"Want to get something to eat?" Spencer asked.

"No. This one is strong. I'm going to go home, sleep it off."

Spencer nodded. When they reached the cemetery's wrought iron gates, they faced each other and leaned forward until their foreheads touched.

"We fight for the stars." Spencer said.

"And the stars for us." Brad replied.

They pulled apart and walked away from each other, Brad went right while Spencer went left. Hints of the morning sun rose over the tip of a mountain as Brad made his way home. Flower gardens spread their scent as bees worked away. A rabbit fled from one side of the street to the other and a bird tweeted through the air. *This planet does have its perks.*

When Brad arrived at the large three-story red brick building, he paused and took a deep breath. *Must not forget who I am. Brad Baker, frat boy, senior at LaPorte University.* He pushed one of the large front doors open and was greeted with the foul scent of old beer and skunk of the ganja. College boys were slumped over couches and on top of the pool table. Last night's rager had been one for the ages. The perfect opportunity for him to sneak out and collect Elizabet's data. His limbs felt heavy as he hauled himself up the three flights of stairs to his room. He entered and shut the door behind him, shrugged off his shoes and fell face first onto his bed before promptly passing out.

Chapter Two
Cumbersome

Elizabet stared at the tree's bark as she clung to it for stability. The tiny grains of wood formed beautiful rivets and irregular patterns; she loved the art of nature. It had rained the night before, releasing the musty scent of the forest. She braced herself, and focused her mind, she was not here, she was somewhere else.

A cool breeze danced along her skin where her dress was open in the back. The sharp sting of the switch brought tears to her eyes. Elizabet would never get used to the shock of that pain and squeezed herself tighter against the tree. *I'm not here.* Her body tensed in rhythm with each hit of the willow tree branch. *I'm someplace else.* The sound of each sharp slap against her flesh flooded into the woods, becoming a part of them.

Father wasn't really her father. Elizabet's parents surrendered her to the church when she was five due to her 'demonic sight'. They believed the church could unburden Elizabet of her wickedness. Father Thomas was the parish reverend assigned to *heal* Elizabet and turn her into a Godly woman. *Good luck with that.* She laughed internally. The dead were a part of who she was, like an extra limb. It wasn't her fault she could see ghosts.

"Breathe, love, just breathe. Tis will be over soon."

Elizabet dared not to respond to, Sarah, the ghost sitting on the forest floor in front of her.

"That's right, child, breathe, almost done now. He's already got a sheen of sweat on his brow." Sarah glared at Father Thomas. "Fat tub o' lard."

Elizabet held back a chuckle and smiled at Sarah, then gave her a curt nod to acknowledge her thanks. If only the others could see what she saw. She ground her teeth against the pain until mercilessly the flagellation stopped. By the end she was hunched over.

"Stand." Father Thomas said. His voice devoid of warmth.

Elizabet lifted her head and turned to face him. His stoic eyes sent a chill down her spine. She clasped her hands together for prayer.

Father Thomas spoke. "Be alert and of sober mind. Your enemy the devil prowls around like a roaring lion looking for someone to devour. Resist him, standing firm in the faith, because you know that the family of believers throughout the world is undergoing the same kind of sufferings. Amen"

"Amen."

"A moment to gather yourself." Father Thomas said sternly before walking away.

When Father Thomas was too far to be seen, Elizabet turned back to Sarah and smiled. "I Peter 5:8-9, a classic, never gets old." Elizabet rolled her eyes. "Wonder when it'll start working to *drive out my demonic sight.*" She said sarcastically.

Sarah laughed. "Probably the same time the ol' cod deems himself a fairy and turns a chatterbox with the squirrels."

Elizabet couldn't help the snigger that escaped her lips causing her to wince in pain. She sucked in the air, grimaced, and leaned against the tree. "I don't know how much more I can take of this. Tis no life."

Sadness wavered on Sarah's eyelids before a ghostly tear slipped down her transparent cheek. "No, tis no life." She wrung her hands. "I've been thinking, love. What if you told them you had a vision from, God."

"What kind of vision?" Elizabet asked.

"Tell them, our holy father has blessed ye with the vision of angels. Your prayer and sacrament had made ye worthy of his love and the town is blessed with his favor."

Elizabet considered Sarah's words. "If they pronounce me a prevaricator I'll hang." Her heart beat rapidly.

"But if they believe ye, they'll build statues in your honor." Sarah said. "Some lies are worth the risk."

Hope blossomed in Elizabets' chest. She could be free of this pain. Honored instead of feared. *Perhaps some lies are worth the risk.*

Loud music forced its way up the stairs to Brad's darkened room. Base rattled the empty glasses on his nightstand. He groaned face down into his pillow and pulled his comforter over his head. Data collection always left him with a mental hangover. His head throbbed as the last days of Elizabets' life faded away. He could almost feel the sting of the cuts on her back. Her scars never did fade and pulled on her skin in the dry winter months. *But she got her statue in the end.* Brad smiled to himself.

He shook his head. *You're not Elizabet, you're Brad, party boy, in the twentieth century*. His stomach protested for attention. *Umm, burrito, must find food*. He rolled out of bed and landed with a heavy thud. Gallegos down the block had the best green chili and they were open twenty-four hours. *Perfect*.

Brad waded through the mess of his room, sniffing shirts and jeans until he found something passable to wear in public. He pulled on his shoes and made his way downstairs. The smooth wood railing and steps formed a spiral to the first floor. He imagined the old Victorian home might have been beautiful once upon a time. Now it was covered in old stains and wooden floors that had become warped from not being properly maintained. A hole in a wall here and there from parties that had gotten out of hand. The university probably spent a fortune to keep the old place standing.

He reached the bottom landing and was greeted with a wave of cheers from three of his roommates.

"He lives!!!" Daniel shouted over the roar of rap music with a drink in his hand that splashed over the rim as he raised his hands in the air.

Brad stuffed his hands in his pockets and smiled. "Yeah, rough couple of nights man."

"Hair of the dog will fix you right up." Daniel yelled in Brad's ear as he slapped him on the back. He snapped his fingers towards another dorm buddy to grab Brad a beer.

"Nah, brother. I gotta grab some grub man, my stomach's gonna eat itself." He roughly curled his fingers into Daniels, pulling him close to pat him firmly on the back. "Later though."

Daniel nodded and threw him gun fingers. "Later."

Brad headed towards the front door and shook off his unease. Daniel gave him the creeps.

Outside the night air was cool and refreshing compared to the stale air of the fraternity house. He pulled his black leather coat tighter and tucked his chin to his chest as he walked. Girls in mini-skirts stared at him as they walked by in groups talking in hushed tones and giggling. Brightly illuminated houses along fraternity row all pumped out their own variety of music.

He hated college life, being surrounded by so many naive people. He missed his last life as a leather worker, making handcrafted saddles, belts, boots and a variety of other specialty goods. That life was simpler, honest. Plus, that body didn't draw as much unwanted attention. *Bonus.* But his opportunities for discrete data collection were limited in that life, so his assessor had him reassigned.

As he rounded the corner headed to the main road, there were more streetlights. He squinted his eyes from the sudden brightness and headed to the storefront three doors down. He opened the door to the Mexican restaurant, Gallegos, and a blast of spicy food smells and homemade tortillas filled his nostrils. It was self-seating here, and Brad tucked himself into a small corner booth.

His server greeted him moments later. "Good evening, what can I get you to drink?" The short brunette smacked her gum and gave him a cheesy grin. *This body gets too much attention.*

He cleared his throat. "Um, yeah, can I get a water and a coke please?"

"Sure thing darlin, be right back." She winked at him as she walked away.

Brad shrugged off his coat and opened the menu on the table. The laminated sheets were sticky and made a sucking noise as he flipped each page. He quickly decided to order his normal smothered burrito and shoved the menu aside.

"Here ya are darlin, water and a coke." The waitress set his drinks down and pulled out a notebook and pen from her apron. "What can I getcha tonight?"

"A beef and bean burrito, smothered in green chili please, all the fixings."

The waitress scribbled down his order then shoved the notebook back into the pocket of her apron. "Coming right up." She smiled again as she walked away.

Brad didn't usually order meat in his burrito, the Stapes bone wasn't the only bone that could transmit life, it was just the most powerful. Meat, even boneless, could transmit faint traces of life. An image here, a feeling there. But his body was craving it.

He propped his elbows on the table and let his face fall into his head, trying to rub the past days of Elizabets' memories from his eyes. When he looked up, Spencer was seated across from him.

"Holy shit!" Brad exclaimed and sat up straight. "I've gotta get you a frickin bell or something. What are you doing here, Spencer?"

"Was your data collection successful?" Spencer asked calmly. He sat rod straight with hands clasped.

Brad took a deep breath and blew it out. "Yeah, it was successful, a full life of data has been stored. When will we deliver?"

"Now." Spencer said simply.

"No. Come on man, let me eat my burrito, I'm starving." Brad pleaded.

Spencer clenched his jaw in annoyance. "Fine. But make it quick."

"You're the best, bro!" Brad leaned across the table to slap Spencer on the shoulder.

Spencer brushed off his shoulder where Brad had slapped him and said. "Please don't call me, 'Bro'."

Brad laughed. "Okay *brochacho*!" and held up his hands in mock surrender.

Spencer sighed but said nothing. Music from a mariachi band across the room filled the silence between them. Minutes later the waitress brought over a steaming pile of food.

"Careful, plate's hot. Can I get you anything else?" She asked.

Brad smiled. "No, thank you."

"And would you like to order anything?" She asked Spencer.

Spencer only shook his head in reply.

The waitress seemed a little peeved by his curtness but smiled anyway before she walked away.

Brad tried to take his time eating his meal, but his stomach cramped in hunger and he practically inhaled the baby sized burrito. He downed his soda and belched loudly before slumping back and rubbing his belly.

"Ah, that's better." Brad said in a satisfied voice.

"Great, let's go." Spencer replied.

Brad left some cash on the table, more than enough to include a good tip, and he and Spencer went back outside to the cold night. They walked around the restaurant to an alley behind the building. They stood next to each and looked straight up to the sky.

"Beam me up Scotty!" Brad joked.

Spencer was not amused. Brad hated this part, it always made him nauseous, and he didn't want to lose the delicious burrito he had just devoured. A low hum vibrated the gravel on the pavement. A soft green light from above enveloped the pair. Suddenly, they hovered just above the ground. As the hum reached ear splitting levels, it stopped. Then they were gone.

Chapter Three
Need A Favor

Brad's senses were muffled, and his breathing halted, as though he were sliding through the dark moist belly of a snake. Claustrophobia sunk in as he endured squeezing pressure on all his sides. The dark was so omniscient that he couldn't tell if his eyes were open or closed. Splotches of dark green and deep blue flashed in sync with a *whomp whomp whomp* sound that increased in speed, until suddenly it all stopped, and oxygen flooded his lungs bringing tears to his eyes. He raised one arm and squinted against a blinding white light. Nausea rolled around his stomach bringing him to his knees.

"Stand up, Brad." Spencer demanded. "The rows are coming."

They were in an expanse of empty white. Far opposite them, pinpoints of red grew larger and larger, as though something was speeding closer. In seconds, white aisles stacked with tiny red boxes surrounded them. A soft ding echoed from somewhere above and one of the red boxes slid out. These were the automated inventory rows. Thousands upon thousands of biological samples sat inside the tiny red spaces.

Brad stood up straight trying to ensure the burrito from earlier did not make a reappearance. He clenched his teeth and swallowed an excess of saliva. He opened his mouth wide and reached his arm down his throat. On the side of his esophagus, just passed his tonsils, there was a tiny pocket. Brad used a finger to peel away the soft flesh and scoop out Elizabets' Stapes bone. He looked at it one last time on the tip of his finger and deposited it inside the open red box. Upon receipt, it closed shut and the aisles swooped away leaving a gust of wind in their wake.

"Ugh. I'll never get used to that." Brad's voice was heavy, and his knees shook. "It's like falling down a mountain and losing a chunk of skin."

Spencer scrunched his face up in disgust. "Do you *have* to be so descriptive all the time?"

"Do you *have* to be so robotic all the time?" Brad quipped.

Spencer only shook his head and was quiet for a moment. "We are fortunate, Brad." He looked at Brad pointedly. "To have been chosen to collect data across the galaxy. The lives we've lived, the information we've been able to gathe r... It's beyond any honor I could have ever imagined. Show a little gratitude."

Brad scoffed. “Easy for you to say, *Spencer*. You’ve never had to be the one depositing the samples. All you have to do is boss me around.”

Spencer squinted his eyes. “Do you need a check-in with an assessor?”

It felt as though Brad’s blood drained from his body, from the top of his head to the tip of his toes, leaving him lightheaded. “N-no. I’m fine. It’s just that they usually give us more time to recoup after a data collection, that’s all.” Brad nervously laughed. “You know how weak these bodies can be.” He gave Spencer a reassuring smile.

Spencer still seemed unsure but said. “Okay.”

A foot away, a waist-high podium rose from the smooth floor. Atop it was a black square, almost like a cell phone or small computer. Spencer strode towards it and tapped a few buttons which brought a large holographic screen to life. Spencer padded his fingers across the screen, his eyes scanning, taking in all the information held there. After a few minutes, he swiped his hand down, closing the screen. The podium returned to the floor as though it had never existed.

“The next data point has been assigned. Next Sunday, nightfall at Travers Cemetery for retrieval.” Spencer said.

“Aye, aye, cap.” Brad mock saluted. “Can we get out of here now, please?”

“You know that’s not how it works; they’ll send us when they’re ready.” Spencer replied with an exasperated voice.

Without warning the ground fell out beneath Brad. As though he were on a falling elevator and being swallowed up in darkness. He tried to stay conscious but failed.

"Bro."

Brad's head was foggy, his whole body stiff, and he was cold.

"Bro. Yo, man, wake up."

Someone kicked him on his side, not enough to hurt, but enough to rouse him. Brad slowly raised his head and looked around. He was out front of the fraternity house, it was dark, and he was laying in the front yard. Grass blades tickled his nose and an ant crawled up one of his legs. He stood up fast and nearly collapsed back to the ground, but someone grabbed hold of his shoulders.

"Dude. One hell of a bender, yeah?"

Daniel kept him upright and actually looked worried for once, it took a lot to phase him. The last time he saw Daniel worried was when a sorority girl drank too much and wouldn't wake up, he dropped her in front of the hospital and took off. No one ever talked about it again. Don't ask, don't tell.

"Um, yeah." Brad cleared his throat and felt strength returning to his limbs. "Thanks, man."

Daniel laughed a sound of relief. “We gotta look out for each other right, brother?”

Brad gave him a half smile. “Yeah, man.”

Daniel patted him on the back. “Come on, Bro. Some of the girls made cookies. Trying to buy their way into the next party.” He chuckled and shook his head.

Brad let Daniel guide him back into the frat house. He hated this place. The smell, the dark, the *untidiness* of it all. He missed his last life... wait. What was his last life again? He was having trouble remembering. He knew he had lived other lives, but now they were nothing more than impressions, and incomplete outlines.

He rubbed his palms on each side of his head trying to clear his headache away. He only needed to remember his next assignment, the rest would come back with time, it must. Next Sunday, Travers Cemetery. He couldn’t let Spencer catch on to any problems or he’d send an assessor. The thought sent chills down his spine. Those thin, too-long green limbs, and probing eyes. *At least I don’t have one of those bodies.*

Brad shook his head and tried to clear the image. Everything was all mixed up, fuzzy. Daniel was shoving a plate of cookies at him as if that would solve all of life's problems. Brad smiled and grabbed one.

“Thanks, man,” Brad said.

“No problem, brother.” Daniel slapped him on the back again. “You should get some sleep, man.” He said as he walked away.

Brad nodded and waited until Daniel went around the corner. There was no way Brad was going up to his room.

He needed to walk, move his body, and clear his head. Something was definitely wrong, but what? Did something go wrong during the return?

Brad shoved the cookie in his mouth and crumbs sprinkled down his front. He wiped his hands on his jeans, brushed the crumbs off his chest, and headed back to the front door. He dug his hands in his pockets for his flip-phone to check the time. 10:40p.m. Perfect. Just enough time to catch the last show of the night.

Something about the smell of popcorn, sickly sweet treats, the sound of carbonated drinks filling up cups, and bright lights in the lobby, all of it combined brought on a sense of calm within Brad. The movie theater was the one place he could always go to escape. No expectations, a place where the world outside would fall away and the pictures on the screen could transport him to a different place entirely, and without all the side effects of data retrieval. Exactly what he needed.

He bought a ticket to the last show, not even bothering to see what was playing. He bought the biggest tub of popcorn and the largest soda. The ticket taker instructed him to the correct theater. The hallway was dimmer than the concessions area. The flat carpet had an ugly multi-colored pattern, probably to hide the stains better. Tiny lights illuminated the floor along each side of the hall. It was quiet. When he reached theater twelve, he grabbed the long silver handle and pulled the large door open while balancing his popcorn and drink with one arm. He nearly lost hold of his stuff but managed to keep his balance. As he entered, he switched one item to each hand and leaned his face into the tub to grab some popcorn with his mouth. The door was slowly closing behind him, but at the last moment, Brad heard a voice shout.

"Hold the door please!"

Brad turned around just in time to stop the door from closing with his foot, his mouth full of popcorn.

She was beautiful. His jaw dropped as she slid through the door, close enough to smell her floral shampoo and see the gold flecks in her brown eyes.

"Thanks." She smiled, her voice smooth and kind, as the door shut behind them both.

Brad blushed and snapped his mouth shut which made him inhale a cluster of kernels. He coughed, spraying flecks of food on the ground.

"Are you okay?" She asked, panic in her voice as she patted him on the back.

Brad hacked and coughed and tried to nod, that yes, he was okay. But the coughing stopped and suddenly he was doubled over trying and failing to pull air into his chest.

She took his tub of popcorn and drink and set it on the ground. Then, she did the unthinkable. She wrapped her slender, warm arms around his torso, fingertips barely reaching his middle, and she heaved on his chest.

Brad coughed one last huge cough and sent the kernels flying. He thought he might die of embarrassment.

"Are you okay?" She asked again, concern and panic edging her voice now.

"Yeah. Yes. Thank you." He tried not to look her in the eyes as he cleared his throat. *Beam me up, Scotty! Now would be great timing.*

She bent over to pick up his refreshments and Brad couldn't help but notice how short her cut-off jeans were. One of her tank top straps slid down her shoulder as she stood up and handed Brad his things. Her long curly hair cascaded down her chest and her smile shone in the darkness.

"Have you seen this one before?" She asked.

Words failed him. *Idiot, say something.* He smiled dumbly and nodded, then paused to let her go up the aisle first. He realized a second too late that he had followed her down the same row. The theater was empty.

She stopped and turned to face him, head tilted, a question on her face.

"Um... are you waiting for someone?"

Bradley, you fucking creep.

"Um, no, sorry. I just, um, do you want to share my popcorn?" *Idiot.* "You know, as a way to say thank you." He tried to give her his least creepy smile.

Relief flooded his whole body when she grinned and laughed and said. "Sure."

She held out her hand to shake, and Brad set his cup in the holder so that he could return the gesture. He couldn't help but notice the little spots of paint on her hands. *An artist, interesting.*

"I'm, Talia." She stated. "Nice to meet you."

"Brad." He replied. "Thanks for saving my life." He nervously laughed.

"Anytime." She chuckled.

They sat next to each other in silence, sharing the tub of popcorn between them. Still, no one else came to the theater. Even when the lights dimmed even further to signal the start of the movie, it was only the two of them. Brad could feel the warmth of her next to him. Tingles ran up his side whenever her arm brushed his. And when she laughed, he thought for sure she would hear his heart beating out of his ribs despite the pounding volume of the movie. He tried to focus on the screen so as to not freak her out. But he couldn't stop himself from stealing glances. The shape of her nose, the curve of her jaw, the way the thin necklace around her neck rose and fell with each breath.

Before he knew it, the movie was over. The lights brightened. His mind began to race. How best to play it cool? *Just ask for her number, you can do that. Use your words, Bradley.* Brad tried to control his breathing as he leaned over to where he had his leather jacket draped over the seat next to him. He pulled his jacket on and gathered his trash, and when he turned back, she was gone.

Chapter Four
Cosmic Love

Brad raced out to the hallway and stopped short when he saw no one. *She probably went to the bathroom.* He realized how unsettling it would be to find a stranger waiting for her and decided to control his emotions and leave the building.

You don't have time for romance anyway.

But the impression of her was seared onto him. She had grabbed hold of him and she wasn't letting go. Something about her felt so familiar, so much like... home.

But you don't even know where your home is.

He tried to shake off the thought of her, of Talia. He turned to the front building exit, and there she was, looking at him with a smile on her face. The golden flakes in her brown eyes danced even more in the light outside of the dark theater.

"Hi." She said with liveliness.

"He-ey." His voice caught partway through, and he had to clear his throat to finish his one word reply.

She stood with her hands behind her back, casually dragging a toe across the ugly multi-colored carpet. "So, um, I don't know about you, but I'm starving, and I'd love some company."

She finished hesitantly and her cheeks blushed. Brad's heart was doing a jackhammer dance in his chest again. *Say something.*

Talia's face winced with embarrassment as the seconds ticked by, and just as it seemed that she might turn and leave, Brad found his voice.

"I know a decent Mexican joint a few blocks away." *Took you long enough.*

Brad couldn't help the grin that spread across his face when Talia instantly smiled brightly.

"Sounds great!" she said.

Talia sucked on her lower lip and released it slowly all while continuing to beam that incredible smile at him, her vibrancy was so overwhelming he had to stare at his shoes as they walked towards the exit.

Outside a strong cool breeze blew through Celia's hair and Brad saw goosebumps rise on her legs and arms as she squeezed herself tight against the cold night. He took his black leather jacket off and wrapped it around her shoulders, then smiled at her and stuffed his hands in his pockets.

She gazed at him sideways with a light in her eyes and said. “Thanks.”

They walked closely and quietly. *She must be as shy as I am.* Every now and again they would bump into each other as they walked along the sidewalk underneath the bright moon, and Brad started to suspect that she was doing it on purpose. As though she was gravitating toward him.

When they reached the brightly lit restaurant, Brad held the door open for Talia and she smiled at him again. He led the way to his favorite fake maroon leather booth and sat down. Talia pulled the jacket off and reached across the table to hand it back to him.

“Thanks again for that.” She said.

He nodded. “You’re welcome.”

He could no longer pull his eyes away as she brushed her fingers through her long curly hair in a ponytail motion, apparently trying to bring some kind of calm to the chaos. She pulled a menu in front of her and scanned it.

“What’s good here?” She asked.

“Not the daily special.” He stated simply.

She laughed. “Why not?”

“Their daily special is just items they have too much of that’s going to expire soon.” He said as he glanced quickly at her and then stared at his menu. *Come on Brad, make eye contact, you’re being a creep again.*

Talia raised her eyebrows in surprise. “Good to know.”

Brad clasped and un-clasped his hands underneath the table as he hunched over the menu that he had already memorized.

Suddenly the table started to shake and Talia laughed. “Oh, sorry.” She blushed again.

Brad looked up and didn’t know what to say. She had been pumping her legs under the table, and that had caused the shaking.

Aren’t we a nervous pair? Say something, Brad.

Brad’s mouth hung open a little when he was saved by the waitress.

“Can I get you something to drink?” It was the same waitress from the other night, she winked at Brad and popped her gum as she looked at him like he was something to savor.

Ugh.

Brad finally made eye contact with Talia, and his heart jumped. “Ladies first.” He grinned.

She returned the smile and her blush deepened. “I’ll have a sweet tea and water please.”

Brad didn’t look away from Talia as he said. “Same.”

The waitress rolled her eyes and walked away.

He sat up straight and brought his hands up to the table, no longer feeling the need to hunch over and hide. “So, are you a student at LaPorte?” Brad assumed most people who appeared in their twenties in this area were students, after all, it *was* a college town.

“I am, Art History major. What about you?” She asked.

“Officially, business major, unofficially, undecided.” He said with a shrug of his shoulders.

Talia softly laughed. “So you don’t know what you want to do after this?”

"Not really, I just kind of do what's expected of me." His voice was deep and solemn.

Talia's brow creased. "That doesn't seem fair. Controlling parents?"

More like a controlling Spencer. "You could say that."

Talia looked at him in a way that was thoughtful, as though she was truly seeing him, and hearing him, instead of just making conversation.

"How old are you?" She asked.

You tell me. Two, three, four lifetimes? Who keeps track anymore.

"I'm a senior." *There, good answer, not exactly a lie.*

Talia narrowed her eyes in thought. "So, what happens when you graduate, and your life is your own? There must be something you want to do?"

I'd like to live a normal human life, one of my own.

"I'd like to open my own restaurant someday." Brad surprised himself. *That felt true, do I want that?*

Talia seemed extraordinarily happy, as though she cracked the code of who Brad was. "That sounds wonderful, Brad."

Something about the way she said his name made his smile falter. *What's my real name? She deserves to know. I deserve to know.*

The waitress brought them their drinks and asked as she set them down. "What can I get ya?"

"Oh um..." Talia stammered and laughed. "I haven't really looked at the menu."

The waitress annoyingly tapped her shoe and it seemed like she was going to walk away to give them more time, when Brad stopped the waitress by holding a hand up and saying to Talia. “Do you have any food allergies or aversions?” He asked as he looked at her. She shook her head. “Do you mind if I order for you?” Brad asked.

She grinned and nodded. “Sure.”

Brad looked at the waitress. “We’ll share a Coctel de Camarones and a shredded beef tostada.” He smiled and handed her their menus.

“Coming right up.” The waitress said as she popped her gum again and walked away.

“What's, Coctel de Camarones?” Talia asked.

Brad perked up. “Oh it’s my favorite.” Images of the sea flashed through his mind. He loved getting impressions of the ocean from eating crustaceans, gliding through the water and seeing things no man has ever witnessed in its mysterious watery depths. Plus, it just tasted good. "Shrimp in a spiced tomatoey kind of sauce with all sorts of ingredients tossed in, like avocado, cilantro, celery, onion, jalapeno.” *You’re rambling, Brad.* He took a breath and laughed at himself. “Anyway, yeah, they put it in a big cup the size of a large bowl and serve it with saltine crackers.”

Talia chuckled, apparently enjoying his enthusiasm. “Sounds awesome, can’t wait to try it.” She paused then looked up at him. “So do you live on campus?”

“No, I’m actually over at Alpha Delta Phi.”

Talia coughed in surprise. “A fraternity guy, huh? I wouldn’t have guessed.”

“Oh really? What’s that supposed to mean?” Brad said with a smirk.

"It's just, well... take our waitress for example, she's obviously very into you, but you've been the perfect gentleman. Most frat guys would be trying to slip a hand up her skirt even though I'm sitting right here. Then there was the whole, 'ladies first' thing, and holding the door open-"

"So what you're saying is, all frat guys are assholes?" Brad said simply.

Talia stammered. "No, I-"

"I'm just kidding." Brad winked. "Most frat guys are assholes."

Talia nervously laughed and Brad noticed that she was twisting her napkin into a miniature rope as she talked.

Talia asked. "So, what did you think of the movie?"

What movie? Oh shit, right. Um, what did we see?

"Yeah, it was really good." Brad said.

"Really?" Talia stared at him quizzically.

Shit, not good I guess?

Before he could stop himself Brad's next words came rushing forward. "To tell you the truth, I just go to the movies to zone out, you know, a break from reality... and after my... *near death experience.*" He said in a mocking tone, paused and lightly chuckled, then looked down at his hands before continuing. "Ya know, you... saving my life, all I could see, all I could focus on, after... was you."

Great, good job Brad, good way to scare her away. What were you thi-

"Me too."

Brad snapped his head up in surprise. "Really?"

"Yeah." She said shyly.

It was as though the air between them electrified, sizzling with energy. Full of desire in their silence. Desire to know more, desire to be closer, to touch.

The waitress suddenly reappeared with a large serving platter holding their food. She set it on the edge of the table and placed their entrees before them. "Coctel de Camarones and shredded beef tostada. Can I get you two anything else?" The waitress asked.

"Um." Brad cleared his throat and looked at Talia, she shook her head and he said. "No, thank you."

"My pleasure." The waitress said as she walked away.

Talia beamed at him. "Show me the ropes, how do we eat this? Is it like a dip thing? Crush the saltines in and eat it like soup?"

Brad's laugh bubbled out of him. "No. Not exactly, you grab a cracker, place a spoonful of the cocktail on top, like so, and-" He took a big bite and said with his mouth full. "Enjoy."

Talia laughed and dug into their meal.

They ate in silence, all while stealing glances at each other. When they were finishing up, Brad noticed that Talia had a dribble of sauce on her chin. Without thinking he grabbed a napkin, leaned over, then slowly and gently wiped her chin. He heard her sharp intake of breath at his touch and looked into her eyes.

"How was everything?" The waitress's voice broke their tension almost as if she were shouting.

Shittiest timing ever, lady.

Talia answered for them. "Wonderful, thank you."

"My pleasure." The waitress said as she placed their check on the table and walked away.

Brad reached for the bill and Talia stopped him when she placed her hand on his. Warmth shot up his arm and his skin almost sparked under her touch.

"My treat." Talia said. "I was the one who invited you." She stated with a smile.

"Thank you." Brad said, and when she pulled her hand away he turned his palm up to brush the tips of his fingers against hers. He could have sworn he saw her shiver, a small smile on her lips.

"How about, on our next date, it'll be my treat?" He asked with a question in his voice.

Talia tilted her head. "Date, huh?" She smiled. "I'd like that."

After Talia paid, they re-entered the clear night together. Brad wrapped his jacket around her again and checked the time. It was late, dangerous to be alone late, so he asked. "Can I walk you home?"

She looked around at the emptiness surrounding them, and said. "Yes, please."

The relief and happiness on her face made Brad want to sing and dance, to pull her close and sway to the music of his heart. He refrained himself as much as he could but was not able to resist the temptation to hold her hand. As he slipped his fingers through hers, she welcomed him. It felt like he belonged there, with her. A sense of comfort that he had never felt before overwhelmed him. Too soon, they came to a stop. It took all his strength to let her go when they reached her apartment.

"Same time next week?" He asked. "I'll pick you up?"

"I look forward to it." Talia grinned and turned to unlock her door, but she hesitated and turned back to face him, she took one step closer leaving barely a sliver of space between them, stood on her tiptoes and touched her lips to his.

Brad's lungs filled with the breath of her and he wrapped his strong arms around her, pressing his lips against hers. The taste of her filled him with unmeasurable peace. When she slowly pulled away from their kiss he had to force himself to let her go.

"Goodnight, Brad."

"Goodnight, Talia."

She went inside and gently closed the door, cutting off the energy of their embrace. Her absence left him cold and he debated on never leaving, just sleeping there by her door until he could see her face again. He shook his head for clarity and forced himself to turn away and head back home. But the image of her, the feel of her, stayed with him.

Chapter Five

The Pot

Brad had scarcely reached the front door of the fraternity house, his feet heavy, exhaustion finally taking hold when Spencer appeared from the bushes around the corner of the house startling him.

"The fuck Spencer?" Brad took a step back.

"Where have you been?" Spencer asked accusingly.

"Dinner and a movie, is that a crime?" Brad said sarcastically.

"I think you need to see an assessor."

Brad gritted his teeth. "No, I don't. I'm fine."

Spencer sighed deeply. "Fine. Our next assignment has been moved up, tomorrow night."

"What?" Brad practically shouted, then lowered his voice and asked. "Why so soon?"

"You know I don't ask questions."

Brad inhaled a frustrated breath. "Whatever, I'll be there. Obviously."

Spencer grabbed Brad's arm, too strong, and said sternly. "Get yourself under control, remember the mission."

Brad clenched his jaw and nodded. Spencer released his arm and stalked off into the night. Brad's eyes bore into Spencer's back as he watched him walk away. Spencer's sudden appearance had Brad shaken and he tried to clear himself of the off-kilter sensation. He couldn't let Spencer recommend him for assessment, he couldn't lose Talia. The image of her swam before him, her golden chocolatey eyes, so innocent, so open. The warmth of her, the taste of her. He couldn't live without it, the feeling that she gave him. Nothing else mattered.

Get the job done, Brad.

The graveyard was eerily quiet. It was dark tonight, the stars and the moon hid, Brad could hardly see his next step. No scuttling, no hooting, or leaves swishing in the trees, the air was still... and stale. *Something is wrong*. Brad's determination pushed him forward even though every sense in his body was screaming at him to run the other way. To run straight to Talia's apartment, confess his true self, and run away with her. *Now's your chance, take it.*

Brad took another step forward and saw Spencer waiting for him next to a headstone. This one, like the last, had a statue as well. Instead of an angel, it was a woman with her arms open wide as if welcoming a crowd to her bosom.

Spencer was unmoving, as stoic as the statue he stood next to. His arms were crossed, and face hidden in the depths of the black hood of his heavy cloak.

"Evening." Brad tried to turn on his charm, but his voice came out croaky and uneven.

"You're late." Spencer did not look at him.

"Are you sure? I think you're early." Brad quipped and laughed uneasily.

Spencer did not reply.

Brad cleared his throat and dropped his forced smile. *Alright, straight to work then*. Brad rolled his sleeves back and crouched down. He placed a fist flat against the earth, pulled back, and rammed his arm toward the ground.

"Ahh, fuck!" Brad jumped up clutching his arm against himself. He danced around trying to shake out the throbbing pain in his hand. "I think I broke my fucking hand. What the fuck?"

"You need an assessment." Spencer stated simply.

Brad's panic bubbled up at his words. He thought about running, but knew it would be no use. They'd be able to find him anywhere. He stopped moving around and nursed his wounds. Spencer knelt down, placed his fist against the ground, pulled back and rammed his arm back down. Massive amounts of dirt sprayed up around him like a wave, clearing the way to the casket below.

Brad took a step back and blocked his head from the flying debris with his good arm. Spencer stood up straight and Brad could have sworn that he had grown a foot. Brad shook under the towering form of Spencer.

"Do your job, Brad."

His voice was all wrong, not human. It had a metallic clang hanging on the edges of his words. Brad's skin crawled and the hairs on the back of his neck rose as he walked past Spencer, he sat on the ground, and lowered himself into the hole. He struggled to lift the lid to the casket and sweat beaded on his forehead from the effort. He finally managed to get a finger under the lip of the lid and eased his good hand in, then used his arm like a lever to lift the top open. Dirt fell away creating a dust cloud around him, which made Brad sneeze and squint his eyes.

When the dust cloud cleared, Brad sifted through the bones until he found the one he was looking for. He opened wide, but couldn't get his jaw to release. Spencer, from above, reached a too long arm down to Brad and roughly forced his jaw to unhinge. Brad swallowed a scream of pain.

"*Take it.*" Spencer growled with his metallic words.

Brad reached a shaky hand inside his mouth and fingered his throat pocket open as Spencer held firmly to his face with his thin pointed fingers. Brad deposited the Stapes bone of Amelia Davis. Spencer slammed Brad's mouth shut and everything went black.

"Amelia!" "Amelia!" "Amelia!" The crowd cried out. Their desperate wails echoed to her ears like nails into her heart, she'd never be able to help them all.

Amelia paced around the large standing room tent; her long dress swished around her ankles creating little puffs of dirt around her feet while she chewed on her nails. She tossed her long blonde braid behind her and put her hands on her hips.

"I can't do this." She gulped. "It'll never be enough."

"It'll be enough for one." Her mother held her tight, rubbing her arms. "And that's all that matters. Just make a difference to one."

Amelia swallowed her uncertainty and marched through the flaps of the tent. The crowd greeted her with their voluminous cheers and idolized sobs, some with their eyes closed clasping their hands tight together in prayer. Amelia took a deep slow breath through her nose. 1... 2... 3... 4... 5... And out through her mouth. 1...2...3...4...5...

She opened her vibrations to the universe before her, as if she were searching the air for emotions, and closed her eyes to focus her mental clarity. She mentally searched for the one most in pain, most desperate and traumatized. When she locked onto a handful of the most hurting people in the crowd, she opened her eyes and searched again for the one that appeared to be the youngest, the one with the most time left to offer the world.

There, him. She pointed a finger toward her target and slowly walked forward as the crowd parted for her like Moses and the sea. A boy, no older than ten, yet as small as a five-year-old being held in the arms of his father. Amelia approached slowly and his father's body started to shake with racking sobs, but he held tight to his son.

Amelia smiled. "Shh, shh, shh, it's okay, he's going to be okay."

Amelia placed a palm on the boy's forehead. His eyes were closed and his breathing shallow and raspy. His pale and clammy skin was almost ashen. She searched for his individual energy, closing out all the other vibrations around her, until nothing else existed in her mind but him, as though he and her alone were in an expansive black room. In her mind she walked toward the boy curled up in the dark.

She kneeled next to him and whispered with a smile in her voice. “I found you.” She smoothed his hair, and he opened his eyes. “Come toward the light with me, leave your pain behind.”

The boy stood with Amelia and blinked, shielding his eyes as the dark room flooded with light.

“There you are.” Amelia laughed with relief and patted the boy's hand. “Live a good life, only for you, no one else.”

Amelia brought herself back to present consciousness. The crowd was praising God and the boy before her was no longer in the arms of his father. He was standing up right with rosy cheeks and a beautiful grin. The crowd began laying hands on her and before long she was swarmed with desperate cries of people begging for her grace.

So many hands clawed on her she fought her way back to the tent where her guard of loyalists made the crowd disperse. Inside the tent, Amelia took two steps to her mother and collapsed into her waiting arms.

Chapter Six

Dreams

Slowly Brad's eyes parted. His vision swam and he tried to hold his head steady to combat the dizziness, but he couldn't move. He felt no straps, yet his body was immobilized. Fear boiled up from his toes to his head until his face was hot from worry. He was in an empty gray room shaped almost like the inside of an egg complete with silky membrane, laying on a raised cold hard slab.

He tried to shout but even his mouth was frozen shut. All he could move were his eyes. They danced back and forth inside his skull trying desperately to see anything around him. An inescapable feeling of disconsolate emptiness overcame him. A tear slid down each side of his face.

Nausea rolled around Brad's stomach, as though the giant gray egg were rotating with him inside it. He squeezed his eyes shut as if that could shut out his disorientation. He tried to count the seconds, but even that was futile as every time he tried the numbers didn't make sense, as if time had no meaning here.

He didn't know how long this went on for, Brad only knew that he'd do anything to make it stop.

Stop.

A figure emerged as if it were able to glide through the shell, spindly and towering. As the figure reached for him, Brad could see its two large black glistening eyes peeping at him from an elongated head. Its skin appeared gel-like, not a solid, yet not a liquid either, the same gray color as the egg walls.

When it reached for him, its skin slowly turned dark green and solid, reptilian. Its' one, long, pointed finger inserted itself into Brads ear. He wished he could scream. Something white like a spiders' web began to lift from Brads feet, and suddenly it was as if his skin were made of thousands of tiny fingernails, and each was being pulled from his flesh.

As the painful web was slowly ripped from his body, Brad began to lose focus; until his consciousness was taken from his body and transferred entirely into the web. Brad, in his web form, floated over his body. The dark green figure with its one long pointed finger was attached to his web, like Brad was some kind of sick balloon.

They left Brad's unconscious body and went through the egg shell, but they did not appear into a hallway, they reappeared in another room, this one black with the sounds of dripping water, like a rotten cave. Hundreds of humanoid sleeping bodies were encased in cylinders of water, air bubbles escaped from their bodies.

They stopped in front of the body of a female. Her dark brown hair, shoulder length and twisted into thick locs, floated in the water around her naked ebony skin, her eyes closed. As they waited there, Brad could see the water inside her cylinder seemed to be dispersing, or perhaps it was the cylinder squeezing in on her as her body absorbed the placenta like tube until only the body was left. Suddenly its eyes and mouth opened wide in noiseless fear, gaping, confused, and terrified.

Brad's web instantly got sucked into the body of the female with even more pain upon reentry then he could have ever imagined. He had no control, and as he realized his mind was leaving him with each inch the body absorbed, he became desperate to escape. To not lose himself.

But his fight was futile, and with one last slurp, Brad was gone.

Chapter Seven

Nothing Else Matters

"What is with you lately?" Talia shouted as she tossed a throw pillow at her roommate.

Angela caught it and threw it back at her face. "Just tired." I have studying to do. Without another word Angela stood from the couch, went to her room, and shut the door.

I hate humans, so needy.

Angela hoped this assignment wouldn't last long. She had just completed orientation. Stathos-6 had guided her through the basics. She was a part of an elite species. Gathering intel from across the universe. Earth was at the highest risk of destroying itself, so they needed as many samples from the planet as possible.

She recalled, when she was seated in the room with the large flashing screens that showed segments from her previous assignments, that the universe was depending on her.

I wonder how old I am.

Stathos-6 hadn't explained how long each of her previous assignments had lasted, so there was no telling. She could either be hundreds of years old, or in her mid-twenties, like her human roommate.

I wonder where I'm from.

Stathos-6 also had failed to mention where her home was. It was almost like she was a blank slate during her orientation.

But that doesn't make sense.

Focus, Angela.

She had a data extraction tonight. She needed to be thinking of her upcoming task, not thinking of herself like a spoiled human.

Angela's thoughts were interrupted by a knock at her bedroom door. Before she had a chance to say, 'go away', Talia barged in.

"Hey, *roomie*, I don't know what's up with you, but you didn't need to throw the pillow at my face."

She stated sternly with her arms crossed, waiting for some kind of explanation, or apology? Angela wasn't sure, but explanation was out, so that left apology.

"You're right, I'm sorry, I also shouldn't have walked away like that. I think I'm not feeling well, you know, finals week, little sleep, and crappy food."

Talia stared at her; confusion etched on her face.

"Finals? Angela, what are you talking about? Finals happened weeks ago. Maybe we should take you to see someone-"

"No."

"But Ange, you're not yourself-"

"I said, *no*. I just need some rest, so if you would please."

Angela got up from her bed and ushered Talia out of her room, then locked the door. She immediately heard Talia slump against it on the other side and heard her say. "Fine, but I'm not letting this go Ange, something's up with you and I'll be here for you when you're ready."

Angela waited until she heard Talia's footsteps recede down the hallway, then shut the blinds of her only window, went to her bed, and rolled herself into the large black satin-backed blanket. She lay there rubbing her temples and cursing this human body.

I bet Stathos-6 never gets headaches.

She was having a hard time remembering her life. Segments of her recent orientation were the only vivid things she could recall. The gray oval room with membrane walls. The large screens that showed her snippets of her life were organic, not like televisions on Earth. Almost as if the room was alive and sharing its thoughts, its data, with her.

Then there was Stathos-6. They started out tall, slender, and Gray like the walls, with two large black eyes that took up most of their head and slug-like skin. But as they placed Angela in the room, they transformed into something more reptilian. Like a large crocodile that walked on two legs, no tail, and an almost human face, if it weren't for all the scales, two slits for a nose, and pointed teeth. The reptilian form color shifted as it communicated with her, not through words, but through thought. Red, purple, blue, back to green and black, like a confused chameleon.

Angela assumed that was her natural form as well, if only she could remember. The feeling of long steel nails in her skull wouldn't go away, the pain made it difficult to concentrate. But she had to be ready for tonight. Despite Stathos-6 explaining that they were her oldest friend and ally, something about them told her that she could not fail.

The cold graveyard pulsed with dark energy; winter was coming. The breeze pushed the leaves around on the ground and chilled her bones. She walked slowly through the aisles of headstones, until finally, she saw them. A dark hooded figure in the distance.

"Statho-"

They held up a hand. "That's not my name on this planet... you will call me, Spencer."

Angela nodded. "Of course, Spencer." If she didn't know any better, she'd say that Spencer looked like the son of some rich and entitled politician. Perfectly styled short blonde hair and bright blue eyes that lacked warmth.

A chill went up her spine. *They could be anyone*. But wait, why would that thought frighten her, she was one of them, *right?*

"Angela, over here." Spencer waved her over to a headstone that was flat in the ground, covered with weeds, and crumbling around the edges.

"How can you tell?" She asked. "I can't even make out a name."

"Are you questioning me?"

The low growl in his voice raised the hairs on her neck. "No, no, of course not, I was just wondering-"

"Don't ask questions that detract from our mission." He glowered at her. "Now, this human body of yours has had some modifications made, but it's mostly mind over matter. You know what to do, go ahead."

Relief flooded through her body when she was able to get to the casket below the ground on her first try. But as she stared at the Stapes bone in her hand, she had to force herself not to gag.

Get the job done, Angela.

"How do these tiny things not disintegrate over time? Shouldn't they-"

Spencer's voice took a new, low, and threatening tone. *"Do not ask questions that distract from the mission, Angela. Now make the deposit."*

Angela's eyes widened in terror. The voice that came out of Spencer was unnatural. She could no longer delay the inevitable, she relaxed her jaw, opened her mouth wide and felt for the small slit inside her throat that she knew could receive the Stapes bone and record the data held on it.

"Good." Spencer said. He roughly pulled Angela's forehead to his and said. "We fight for the stars."

"And the Stars for us." She replied as her skin crawled with unease.

Angela bit back her tears that she didn't fully understand as she watched Spencer walk away.

Her flesh was burning, slowly but surely there'd be no jacket left. She pulled and pulled against her crisscrossed bound arms, but it was no use, the white straitjacket wouldn't budge. She accidentally leaned back a quarter of an inch and was rewarded with another burn on her back. These sadistic nurses left her tied to a radiator heater two days ago, but they were stupid enough to use a tether this time instead of chains. If she could just get the angle right and burn a hole through the tether, then she'd be able to break free.

She twisted her body a little to the left and leaned back again. She heard a very faint sizzle, the sound of fabric frying, and prayed it was the right bit of fabric this time. She counted to thirty, and waited for the feeling of burning skin, but it didn't come.

Yes! Just a few more seconds.

Suddenly she fell against the cold hard tile floor.

I did it!

She hurriedly freed herself from the fabric imprisoning her body and tossed it to the ground. Her knees and back were stiff as she stood. She rubbed her thighs to try and get some blood flow moving through her lower extremities. She looked down and saw her pee-stained white pants.

I need to find some clothes.

But that would require going into the employee only wing of the 'hospital' and that was a definite no. She'd have to find something on the streets.

Clara knew the dark side of the city better than most considering her mother tossed her out of the home when she was fourteen. She did well for herself, lied about her age and lived at a shelter while she finished high school. But then she had her first, very public, *episode*, during her first semester at college and ended up in this place. Clara couldn't handle one more zap to the brain, or being forced into ice cold water until her lungs almost gave out. She couldn't live with torture.

Her bare feet padded softly against the floor as she slowly made her way through the darkened corridor. The sounds of the insane asylum inhabitants made her skin crawl, as if they were no longer human the longer they were trapped here. She brushed a lock of hair out of her face and almost cried at feeling how matted it was, she'd probably be forced to shave her head.

Clara's pulse quickened when she finally saw the green glow from the illuminated exit sign. She walked as quickly as she dared, scared to make too much noise. She saw nothing else, heard nothing else but the exit sign and the faint buzz it emitted. Her mouth twitched up at the corners with hope, freedom was mere inches away.

She reached for the push bar of the door when she was forcibly tugged back.

NO.

Her eyes widened in terror, and she tried to scream but her mouth and nose were covered with a heavy wet cloth.

"Where do you think you're going." A sadistic deep voice growled at her.

The man was easily double Clara's size and smelled of onion. Her eyes were becoming heavy, and her body weak. No, *no no no*... "NO!!!"

Clara screamed out shrill and desperate and the man was flung back off his feet. The light bulbs in the ceiling lit up for a moment then popped and shattered, spraying glass all along the ground. The guard was unconscious and had blood dripping from his nose and eyes. Clara's chest pounded with adrenaline. An alarm rang out and the halls echoed with the animal-like screams of the other inhabitants locked in their cells.

Clara's breathing came out fast and harsh, she took one last look behind her and sprang for the door. Blinding sunlight assaulted her, and Clara held a hand in front of her face to block its rays. She hesitated for only a moment, and then ran.

Angela rubbed the crust from her eyes as the last images of Clara's life left her mind. Clara lived a full and unremarkable life. Living off the grid but finding peace in nature and was never locked up again. She was eighty years old when she had a heart attack close to town. She was buried as Jane Doe.

Those abilities didn't make sense. A *human shouldn't be capable of that.* Angela rubbed her temple as she tried to make sense of what she had seen in her mind. Why did Spencer-no, we, why did *we* need this information?

She tried to shake off the feeling that something wasn't adding up.

Something is wrong.

Chapter Eight

Slide

The days passed slowly after Angela relived the life of Clara. She had expected Spencer to call upon her immediately to deposit Clara's Stapes bone on the mothership, but he hadn't yet called on her to turn the information over; and the longer she held onto it, the more she felt that Spencer shouldn't possess the information.

Something within the deep recesses of Angela's mind was telling her to protect the information at all costs. But once they called on her to turn it over, how would she deny them? But did that mean she was betraying her own kind? A traitor to her people? But was she a person? Were they people? Did they possess souls?

They were collecting samples to save the planet, right? Why would she want to go against that kind of goodness?

She couldn't explain it, and she didn't have all the answers, but somewhere deep within herself, like a tickle at the back of her brain, a small voice was guiding her; and that little voice was the only one she trusted wholeheartedly.

Pounding on her door reprieved her of her inner turmoil.

"Angela!" Talia pounded on the door again. "I need you! I need my best friend."

Angela groaned from the effort of pulling herself out of bed, how long had she been there? She reluctantly shuffled to the door and opened it a crack.

Talia jammed a foot in the opening as if Angela might slam it shut at any moment. She peered behind Angela into the darkened room.

"Woah." Talia covered her mouth and nose with her hand. "Okay, you definitely need this as much as I do."

"Need what?" Angela asked as she tried to keep the annoyance out of her voice.

"We're kicking some ass!" Talia stated proudly and resolutely.

"What?" Angela's brow creased together in confusion. "Whose ass are we kicking?"

Talia pushed her way past Angela and yanked open her window blinds to let the moonlight in. "I've had my heart broken Ange, and you're going to help avenge me."

"Okay, is this some kind of role-playing thing? I'm not into that, Talia. I just want to sleep."

Talia rifled through Angela's drawers for clean clothes as she spoke. "No, I'm being serious. I met this guy the other night and we were supposed to have a second date tonight, but he stood me up!" She tossed a pair of jeans and a loose short sleeve shirt onto the bed. "Now... normally, I'd let it go, blow it off, 'get under someone new!' you know, all that bullshit. But, I felt some kind of way about this guy and I'm not going to let him ditch me without some kind of explanation." She practically shrieked as she explained herself, waving her arms in the air as if that could help get her point across. "I also wouldn't normally drag you into my retribution story, but Ange, you're in a dark place, literally *and* figuratively. You need to shower, brush your teeth, eat something, breathe fresh air. So, I'm recruiting you, I'm not taking no for an answer, and you're going to have my back, like a best friend should!"

Angela's head spun from the sudden onslaught of her roommate. "Um. Okay. Well just give me a minute to get dressed-"

"No. I'm sorry, Ange, but you stink. Shower, teeth, food, then we confront!"

Talia grabbed a towel hanging on a hook on the back of the door and shoved it into Angela's hands, and practically pushed her out of the room toward the bathroom across the hall.

Talia shoved her in and slammed the door. "Twenty minutes Ange!" She shouted from the other side. "Then, we ride!"

Angela couldn't help but smile. Talia was crazy, but she was *her* crazy. Something about that woman stirred something deep within her, like that little tickle at the back of her brain, only this was like a tiny spark in her heart.

Thirty minutes later they were walking outside to go get something to eat. It was a clear cool night. Various businesses along the main street stayed open late to accommodate the night owl students who lived here, one of the perks of living in a busy college town. Conversation from other people filtered in and out of her ears as they made their way to wherever Talia was leading them.

Talia's long strides were hard for Angela to keep up with. "Hey, Talia, you realize not all of us have super model legs, right?"

"Huh?" Talia glanced behind her and slowed down when she realized that Angela was practically running to keep up. "Sorry, Ange, just kind of worked up, ya know?"

"Not really, no. But I support you anyway." Angela winked and was rewarded with one of Talia's cute grins.

They reached the doors of the brightly lit Mexican restaurant, and when Angela held the door open the smells of delicious handmade food made her stomach cramp in hunger.

How long has it been since I ate something?

There was a sign on a small table that said, SEAT YOURSELF, so they maneuvered their way around the tables to a small booth near the back. They removed their jackets as they sat down opposite each other and opened the menus already on the table.

"So, where'd you find this place?" Angela asked.

"It's where *he* brought me that night. The food is amazing, but..." Talia hesitated and glanced up to look at Angela. "I was also kind of hoping to run into him here."

"Oh, Talia, babe, you got it bad, don't you?"

Talia shrugged her shoulders and kept looking at the menu. Angela reached across the table to hold Talia's hands. "Hey, we'll be stalkers together. Dude won't know what hit him!" Angela winked and laughed. They both knew she was being sarcastic, playful. Talia wiped a tear from the corner of her eye as she laughed too, and Angela had the sudden urge to move to her side of the booth and wrap her arms around her in comfort, so she did just that.

Talia let out a wet laugh as Angela embraced her. "Since when are you so maternal?"

"What? I can't comfort my best friend?"

Talia shrugged away from Angela's hug with another laugh, and Angela thought her heart might crack.

"No, it's not that." Talia said. "It's just not like you. You're usually the one saying, shake it off, and toughen up. Something really is up with you, Ange."

You have no idea.

Angela shyly went back to her side of the booth and tried to think of something snarky and motivating to say, to recover from her apparent fou pas. But nothing came to mind. Instead, she was saved from her embarrassment when the waitress came by to get their drink order.

Gratefully for Angela, Talia didn't seem to notice any tension. After the waitress left, Talia said. "So, this guy let it slip that he's part of the fraternity over at Alpha Delta Phi, I figure we go over there after this and let him have it!"

Angela forced a chuckle. "Okay, as you wish."

Talia tilted her head and squinted her eyes. "As I wish? Geez Ange."

Talia laughed and shook her head and Angela thought she might die of embarrassment as her cheeks flooded with warmth.

After a very quick and quietly awkward dinner, they were headed to the frat house. Talia didn't seem to notice how deeply Angela's inner torment went. She did all the talking for the both of them as they walked. Talia seemed to realize that Angela wasn't herself, but she had no idea how accurate that was.

Angela couldn't make heads or tails of her own emotions. She didn't feel like a *non-human.* The opposite in fact, she had never felt more alive, and she was fairly certain that Talia was the cause. Angela caught herself cataloging everything about her as she stole glances along their walk.

The way Talia's long hair was shorter around her face, the way her curls bounced as she walked, the way the tiny flakes of gold in her eyes shimmered like dust in the air. Then there was her smile, the way her heart-shaped lips tugged Angela's eyes to them, and the way her voice sounded like a song no matter the tone.

The longer they walked, and the more pain Angela saw etched on Talia's face, the more Angela wanted to burn the world down. This *guy*, whoever he was, would regret ever hurting *her* girl.

Talia stopped abruptly. "We're here."

Angela watched her take a shaky breath and said. "You know, we don't have to do this if you don't want to."

Talia clenched her fists. "No, I need to. I need to know why."

Angela nodded in understanding. "Okay, let's do this then."

Angela followed a foot behind as Talia marched up to the door and knocked as hard as she could three times. Angela stood with her arms crossed and face set like stone, ready to back up *her girl.*

Laughter and footsteps sounded from the other side of the heavy oak door. A tall skinny guy with pooka shells around his neck, who looked like he belonged at a beach answered the door.

"Ah, yeah, can I help you?"

Angela watched as Talia's hands shook slightly, she seemed to be losing her nerves. Angela spoke up for her. "Yeah, we're looking for someone who lives here."

Beach guy looked Angela up and down, slowly, like he was tasting her with his eyes and liked what he was seeing. Angela shivered with disgust.

Beach guy leaned against the doorframe coolly and said. "Well, you found me, what can I do for you?" He bit his lower lip and Angela thought she might vomit.

Talia seemed to find her voice. "Okay perv, take it easy, we're looking for Brad."

Beach guy seemed to turn off his charm. "Oh." He turned around and shouted into the house. "Brad! You got company!"

A minute later, more footsteps sounded, and beach guy moved out of the doorway. Brad took his place in the doorway. He was gorgeous, and Angela could understand why Talia was so smitten with him.

"Uh, yeah, can I help you?" He asked in a pleasantly deep voice that rolled like silk.

Talia stammered. "It's me...Talia."

Brad looked confused and didn't say anything.

Talia's cheeks flamed red as she said. "We had a date tonight! You stood me up!"

Brad laughed. He *actually, laughed*, at *her* girl. Angela wanted to rip his throat out with her teeth.

"Look, I'm sorry, but you got the wrong guy, I've never seen you before in my life... and, you're not exactly my *type*."

Yep, frat boy needs to die.

Tears welled in Talia's eyes as Brad turned back into the house. Angela thought she might follow him inside and kick

Brad in the nards, but Talia walked away, went back toward the sidewalk and Angela followed her.

Seconds later they heard footsteps slapping on the pavement behind them, and a needle tore at Angela's heart when she saw Talia's disappointment, it wasn't Brad, but beach boy chasing after them.

"I swear to God, if you say one more dumb ass thing I'll slap you so hard you won't be able to talk for a week!" Angela shouted at him.

"Woah." Beach boy laughed. "Take it easy killer." He held his hands up in surrender. "I come in peace."

"What do you want?" Talia glared at him.

"Look." He cleared his throat and shoved his hands in his pockets. "Normally I wouldn't meddle in my boys' affairs, but you seem really hurt by this."

"Get to the point pooka shells." Angela snarled at him.

Beach boy gave her a look that chilled her bones and Angela almost regretted her insult.

"The *point*, is-that my boy hasn't been himself lately. I mean, he is now. But he doesn't remember the last two weeks."

Angela was surprised by the sincerity in beach boys' voice.

"Whatever, you're just trying to cover for him." Talia said.

"No. Really. I even found him passed out in the yard a couple times. And last week one night he came home looking like the happiest person on Earth." Beach boy took a breath. "Honestly, I think that was the night he met you. But as of a few days ago, he's back to his old self. I really don't think he remembers you." Beach boy shrugged and turned to head back to the house. "Sorry." He shouted over his shoulder.

Angela watched Talia stare at his back as he walked away with her mouth hanging open.

"Well, that didn't go exactly as I imagined." Talia said. "I can't believe he doesn't remember me. I even saved his life!"

Those words were like an electric shock to Angela's brain. She stopped in her tracks as the memory came flooding back. Talia's arms hugging her middle and giving the Heimlich to get the stuck kernels out of her throat. Sitting next to her in the movie theater. Watching her every move. Dinner after. And that kiss. That world spinning, never want to let go, world changing kiss.

That was me. I'm Brad.

Shit.

Chapter Nine

Teardrop

It was as if Talia were talking to her through water. Angela felt dizzy, the world spun.

I was in Brad's body before this one. I'm the reason Talia is heartbroken.

Her mind raced, petrified about what else she didn't remember. She thought the mothership had shared everything of importance to the mission with her, but now, everything she knew was uncertain, unmoored like a boat lost at sea being thrashed in the waves.

Angela already knew she was missing key pieces of information, like how old she was and who her original self was. But that wasn't necessary to complete the job at hand. This, however, seemed like something she should know.

How could they possibly not tell her a key piece of information, like the fact that she's living in the same town as her previous assignment? If Brad had recognized Angela, it could have triggered his memories, he could have recalled his time on the mothership when her consciousness was taken from Brad's body and put into this one, and then her cover would be blown.

And why this body? It couldn't be a coincidence that she was now Talia's roommate. Did they know about Brad and Talia's encounter? Was Talia in danger? She would never forgive herself if anything happened to Talia.

"Angela."

An unfamiliar emotion coursed through Angela's veins. The little hairs on her arms stood to attention. An involuntary shiver shot up her back as if someone had poured ice down her shirt. Pictures of Talia's body laying on a cold hard slab were suddenly flashing through her mind.

"*Angela!*"

The image of Talia being experimented on, defiled, samples taken...

"ANGELA!" Talia grabbed Angela by the shoulders firmly and shook her free of her tortured thoughts. The clouds behind Angela's eyes cleared and she was brought back to the present.

Talia's face was overtaken by fear, her eyes wide, breathing rapidly, gaze darting back and forth across Angela's face as if searching for the thing that was stealing her away.

"What was *that*?" Talia demanded.

"I'm sorry, I guess I just zoned out for a sec." Angela replied.

Talia clenched her teeth and swallowed multiple times as though her mouth had gone dry. She looked all around them to see if anyone was watching them. After a few moments she responded in a hushed tone. “No. Your eyes literally clouded over and your body was hovering like two inches off the ground, Ange.”

Uh oh.

Words failed her, all that came out of Angela’s mouth were a few mumbled sounds. Panic began to pull her into her mind again when a sudden sharp smack stung her across the face.

Haha, she slapped me! Damn. That was kind of hot.

“Wake the fuck up, Ange!” Talia shouted and let out a deep breath of air, before her eyes darted around them again. She huffed and crossed her arms, standing defiantly before saying. “Now you’re going to tell me, *exactly what.i n.the.fuck. Angela.* Right now. Or I’m dragging your ass to a hospital.”

What do I say? Fuck. Fuck. Fuck.

“I’m waiting, *Angela*.” Talia spoke through her teeth.

“Um...” Angela stammered. *Say something*. Angela looked around them and shrugged her shoulders. “Maybe we can chat about this at home?”

They were still standing on the sidewalk in front of the fraternity house’s sprawling front lawn.

Talia seemed to take in their surroundings and nodded her head. “Yeah, that’s probably best.” She hesitated and narrowed her eyes at Angela before saying. “But we’re making a stop on the way home. This night calls for massive amounts of ice cream." She stalked off, her long curls bounced as she walked.

Angela smiled and followed her.

After walking in silence for a couple of blocks, Angela hurried to catch up to Talia.

Angela looked at her sideways and grinned before saying. "You know, you're pretty cute when you're all worked up."

Talia lurched to a halt and stared at Angela quizzically. "Cute?"

Angela only smiled and shrugged.

Talia's mouth quirked up at the corner as if she were fully digesting the word and it was settling pleasantly in her stomach. At least, that's how Angela interpreted her slight tilt of her head and blush of her cheeks.

The ice cream parlor was a kitschy place. The exterior of the double doors was fashioned into the shape of two giant ice cream cones complete with three scoops of plastic strawberry on top. Angela followed Talia inside to be greeted by the sweet scent of waffle cones and the loud whir of three large open chest freezers working overtime to keep the space cool. The brightly lit interior was adorned with old fashioned forest green high-backed booths and black and white checkered floors.

"Quaint." Angela smirked.

Talia nudged her, serious at first and clearly still mentally processing what she had just seen, but the longer Angela smiled at her, the more the crease in Talia's brow went away.

Then Talia said. "Yes, it *is* cute. Plus, everything is *home-made.*" Talia raised one eyebrow and smiled as if that sealed the deal that this place was legit the best.

It was a quarter to closing time and they were the only customers in the store. Angela watched in admiration as Talia strutted confidently up to the counter and ordered.

The employee seemed to be close in age to them, mid to late twenties. His auburn straight hair hung haphazardly across his forehead and he most definitely was making eyes at Talia. Angela glared at him as he stared at Talia and he said. "Well hello, ladies. What do I have the honor of making for you two beauties tonight."

Ugh, barf.

Talia gave him a courtesy smile and small chuckle. "Yeah, um, can we please get the custom vanilla bean gallon with black cherries, caramel, cookie dough, and cheesecake bites mixed in please?"

He winked and Angela had the sudden urge to steal his tip jar out of spite when his back was turned, but she refrained.

"Coming right up he said over his shoulder as he scooped their toppings.

Talia turned away from the ice cream bar to face Angela, leaned in and whispered. "*What* is with the evil glare?"

Angela took a step closer and whispered back. "I don't like the way he's looking at you."

Talia laughed out, loudly, sharp, and unexpected, then hurriedly slapped a hand across her mouth to stifle the sound. When she composed herself she said. "What are you now, my bodyguard, Ange?"

Angela lowered her eyes and shrugged without saying anything.

A few minutes later the employee reached over the plastic sneeze guard to hand Talia her gallon of ice cream.

"That'll be $11.84 please." He said.

Talia dug into her purse and pulled out a ten and a five, handed it to him, and said, "Keep the change."

He smiled and replied. "Thanks ladies, have a wonderful night."

As they left the parlor and entered back into the shelter of the night, Angela pondered what it was about Talia that evoked such strong reactions. Her rational mind knew she was being a little, *over-protective*, but her emotional mind saw every person who showed even a remote interest in Talia as a threat. Angela realized that she really needed to take it down a couple notches, but everything right now felt off balance and the only thing keeping her solidly on her feet was Talia.

Angela's only goal, only focus, was being Talia's shield, because she felt that it was inevitable that the world would eventually come crashing down around them.

They finally made it back to the apartment. Talia shrugged off her jacket and let it fall to the floor. Angela scooped it up and hung it on the coat rack before taking her own black leather jacket off and hanging it next to hers. Angela heard Talia rummaging around in the kitchen for bowls and spoons, as cupboards clapped, and drawers slammed shut.

Fuuuck-she's upset. Well, duh, what'd you expect, you fucking hovered dumb ass.

Talia stomped out of the kitchen, plopped on their brown velvet couch, sat cross-legged, and shoved a large spoonful of ice cream into her mouth. After loudly swallowing she looked at Angela and said. "Okay, I'm ready. Lay it on me. What in the actual fuck, Ange?"

Angela hovered near the entryway, and hesitated, unsure on how to answer that. Any lie she could come up with would be just as unbelievable as the truth, so she settled on that, the truth.

Angela slowly made her way to the couch, sat next to Talia, and took a deep breath.

"I'm not... Angela." She said.

Talia laughed and rolled her eyes. "Come on, Ange. I'm being serious. What was that back there? Some kind of seizure?"

Angela clasped her hands between her thighs and chewed on her bottom lip. Finally, she looked up at Talia, and held her gaze. "Talia. I am inside Angela's body, but Angela is not here right now."

Talia laughed again, so much so that she snorted and spit out a little bit of her ice cream. When Angela didn't respond, Talia sat up a little bit more straight and swallowed hard.

"Um, Ange, I think maybe we should call someone."

"No." Angela replied sharply.

Talia leaned away from Angela as though she were scared. "Listen, Ange, you're freaking me out."

The last thing she ever wanted was to scare her. Desperation clawed at her inside to be believed. "Talia. I would never do anything to hurt you." Angela said and reached urgently for Talia's hand.

Talia pulled her hand out of reach and leaned away. "Yeah, sure. That's what all the murderers say right before they murder. You're obviously in some kind of mental health crisis, Angela!"

Talia un-crossed her legs and stood up fast, clinging to the bowl she held as if she could use it for a weapon if she had to. Angela could tell that Talia was trying to control her voice but it still came out shrieky.

Angela stood slowly with her hands out as if to say, 'I mean you no harm', as though Talia were a wild animal prime to run off at the sound of any twig snapping in the distance.

"Talia. Please. How do you explain what you saw?" When Talia didn't move, Angela continued talking cautiously. "You said yourself, I haven't seemed like *me* lately. Please. Give me a chance to explain."

Talia shook her head, eyes wide, ready to run, but held steadfast and said. "Fine. I won't make any calls tonight. But I'm not saying I believe or understand you. I need some space, Ange."

Angela nodded. "I understand."

Talia slowly walked backward to the direction of her room, turned at the last second as she sequestered herself in her room, and Angela's heart sank to her knees when she heard the click of the lock on Talia's door.

Chapter Ten

It's Been Awhile

The next morning it took all the restraint that Angela possessed to keep herself from waiting inches from Talia's door. Talia needed space and she was going to honor that by not freakishly standing by her room like an obsessed puppy slobbering at the mouth. Angela paced the short length of her bed again and again until her footsteps were permanently ingrained into the carpet.

Angela was sure that centuries from now historians would discover this spot and declare, 'Here lies the place where someone was surely tortured to death.' because that is precisely how waiting felt to Angela. Each tick of the clock on her wall was an annoying reminder that time passed far too slowly for her liking.

Tick.

Tick.

Tick.

"Ugh! Make it end!" Angela shouted under her breath and pulled at her hair before sighing deeply and falling backward onto her comforter. She lay there, feeling the pulse of her heart, her human heart, pumping blood through this body. Each breath calmed her deeper and deeper into a sense of sanity-until her mind wandered back to Spencer.

Where was he? Surely the data she held should have been collected by now. His absence left an unsettling void in her chest. Something was wrong, *that*, Angela was sure of.

The click of a lock pulled Angela from her thoughts. She strained her ears to listen as Talia left her room. Footsteps padded on the carpeted hallway. The bathroom door creaked open, then shut. Then, the sound of running water. Angela began to pace again. Should she give more space? Stay in her room? Her nerves couldn't take the uncertainty. She decided to be as open and calm to whatever Talia's reception of her may be today. She also decided that it may help *sway* her likability by being a good roommate. For a start, she would make Talia's favorite comfort food, pancakes.

Angela cautiously opened her bedroom door and peeked out. The bathroom door across the hall was still shut. She made her way to the small living room with an open view of the kitchen. The two spaces were separated by a short bar with two barstools.

Angela entered the kitchen and started taking down mixing bowls and pulling out eggs, flour, and the other ingredients she would need.

She spoke to the smart device hooked up to their small apartment. "Hello Otto. Play Talias' playlist."

"Playing, Talias' playlist." It replied in a robotic voice.

Angela danced around the small kitchen barefoot as she mixed, taking an extra deep whiff of the vanilla before she added it in. She turned the skillet on medium high and cut a tablespoon of butter onto it. Before long the savory sizzle of margarine filtered to her nose. She was flipping the second batch of pancakes when Talia's sweet voice rang in her ears.

"Pancakes, huh?"

Angela twirled around to see Talia's combed wet hair dripping down the front of her flannel Pj's.

Talia's lips quirked up into a small smile when she said. "Trying to suck up to me I see." She said with a knowing grin.

Angela gulped and cleared her throat. "I just thought maybe you might be hungry." She shrugged.

"Well, don't just hoard em, pass them on over here."

The light in Talia's eyes instead of fear gave Angela far more hope than she felt she deserved. She could feel her heart beating again as she passed the plate full of pancakes and bottle of syrup over to Talia who was sitting at the kitchen bar.

Too scared to push her luck, Angela smiled then turned back around to finish cooking the last of the batter.

"Playing my playlist too, huh? I thought you hated my music? Called it-what was it you said? Auto-tuned crap?"

Angela stiffened and then relaxed when she heard Talia's laugh. She chuckled in return and said. "I just thought you would appreciate it."

Every silence, no matter how small, sent Angela's pulse racing.

One.

Two.

Three.

Talia's beautiful voice. "Well, you thought right. Thanks, Ange."

A deep breath.

One.

Two.

"You're welcome."

A smile.

One.

Angela placed the last of the pancakes onto the large serving platter, grabbed her own smaller plate and filled it. *We're eating together.* She couldn't stop the smile that spread across her face. She felt like pumping a fist into the air and dancing.

When they were finished, Angela gathered their plates and took them to the sink to wash. She watched out of the corner of her eye as Talia got comfy on the couch and put a live news channel on the television. Angela smiled again. *She didn't retreat to her room.*

When Angela was done cleaning up, she stood uneasily in the kitchen, until Talia said. "Do you need an invitation?"

Angela laughed in relief and slowly made her way to the opposite end of the couch and sat down.

Talia muted the TV and turned to face Angela, scooping her legs up to sit criss-cross, then said. "So. Let's talk about last night."

Angela's fingertips tingled and she had the urge to bounce a foot up and down nervously. She didn't know where to start, what to say first? There was so much undiscovered territory to cover here.

She was reprieved from talking when Talia spoke again.

"So, you aren't Angela. But you're in Angela's body. And you claim you're not in a mental health crisis."

Angela could only nod her head in agreement. So many words were stuck in her throat.

Talia continued. "Look, Angela is my best friend, and I would absolutely put her health as a priority, but I can't explain the hovering, or the clouded over eyes. That's not exactly a *normal* thing, and you haven't seemed to be a threat. That's the *only* reason I haven't called the police or an ambulance, and it's the only reason I'm going to give you a chance to explain."

Angela finally was about to find her voice when Talia kept talking.

"*But*. One false move, and I'm calling the cops. Understood?"

Angela nodded her head fiercely before saying. "Uh huh, yes, absolutely, understood."

One.

Two.

Three.

Four.

Say something.

"Um... so... I'm not Angela. But I'm also not really sure who I am."

Talia squinted her eyes. "What do you mean? Where is Angela? Is she dead? Are you a ghost? Did you possess her?"

Angela's eyes widened and she shook her head. "No-".

Talia interrupted her. "And what do you mean, you don't know who *you* are?"

Angela laughed internally when Talia used her fingers for air quotes on that last question.

Feeling a little calmer and surer about herself, Angela said. "Why don't I tell you what I *do* know?"

Talia seemed to be nodding and shaking her head at the same time as she clasped her hands together and said. "Sure. Why not."

Angela cleared her throat and started. "I'm not a ghost. I woke up on the mothership-"

Talia snorted, then promptly erupted into laughter. "Wait-wait, wait, wait." She laughed so hard and long that she began gasping for air. "Mothership?" More laughter. "You mean like, *take me to your leader.*" She said mockingly with her arms straight out like a zombie. "Aliens. You're saying you're an alien?"

Angela gave her a stone-cold stare and remained quiet.

Talia stopped laughing and sat up a bit straighter. "Okay. Prove it. Prove to me that you're an alien."

Angela took a deep breath then let it out slowly, thinking of what she could do to prove herself. Blasting a hole through the floor with her super strength probably wasn't the best idea. After a few moments of silence, she had decided what to do. She wiggled her jaw side to side until it unhinged. She stretched her mouth wide open, reached her hand inside her mouth, pulled the little flap open and pulled out Claras' Stapes bone.

Talia shot off the couch like she had seen a giant spider and screamed. She jumped around waving her arms and rubbing her body free of the heebie jeebies.

"What the fuck!" She shouted. "What in the actual fuck?" She yelled again and turned away from Angela as she desperately grabbed at her skull through her curls as she bounced around.

Angela calmly put her jaw back in place and held the Stapes bone on her open palm. She waited until *finally* Talia quieted and cautiously, step by step, made her way back to the couch.

Talia started to speak but her voice caught in her throat. She tried again and said almost in a whisper. "So. Aliens. You're an alien. Okay." She took a deep breath, "And what is *that*?"

"It's a Stapes bone." Angela simply stated.

"No. It's not. human bones aren't golden." Talia said.

For the first time Angela realized she was the one getting new information. She tilted her head and asked. "What do you mean?"

Talia grabbed Angela's wrist to pull her open palm closer for a better look. Angela's skin warmed under her touch and her heart flip flopped. Talia grabbed her phone off the table, and for a split-second Angela was scared she was making due on her promise to call the police; but instead she kept tapping at the screen. A few seconds later she held up a picture of a human Stapes bone.

"Yeah, you see, that's the same size and shape of a Stapes bone, but human ones are definitely not gold. Also, how old is this? It'd have to be *pretty fresh* if it was human."

Talia paled. "And where did it come from?" She leaned away. "Are you going to eat me?"

Angela's eyes widened in terror. "*What*? No. Never. Oh my god you've got it all wrong."

Angela placed the bone on the coffee table and reached for Talia but stopped when she saw fear in Talia's eyes. She scooted back to the far end of the couch and said. "This bone is from a grave that was decades old. They store the entire life of the person it belonged to, like a biological hard drive. I gather them and file the data."

Talia seemed to relax, if only a little. "Yeah, definitely not a human bone, that thing would have disintegrated a long time ago."

Angela digested this information and wondered to herself, if not human, then what kind of data was she collecting?

Talia interrupted her thoughts. "So, where *is* Angela?"

Angela looked at her. "I'm sorry, but I don't exactly know." She paused and when Talia didn't say anything, she continued. "The bodies seem a little bit like blank slates when I enter them, but I slowly take on bits of their personality and memories. I'm not sure if their consciousness is removed for the length of inhabitation, or just dormant, like put to sleep while I'm in here. And after meeting Brad the other day, it seems they don't remember anything from my time being in their bodies."

Talia's mouth hung open, her eyes disbelieving what she was hearing.

Talia's voice was so small when she said. "Wait, what do you mean, 'after meeting Brad the other day?' Are you?... you're who I went on a date with last week? You're the one who I gave the Heimlich to?"

"Yes."

Talia stood and began to pace again. "Okay. Okay. *This is a lot.*"

"There's more." Angela said.

Talia let out a maniacal chuckle. "Of course there's more!" She shook her head and continued to pace.

When I woke on the mothership, the ship told me that my species was collecting information from your planet because your species was slowly killing the Earth. I was also told that I was assigned the important task of collecting the samples, and that this wasn't my first body. After meeting, Brad, I remember some time spent in his body, and I vaguely remember one other body before that. But they didn't tell me, and I don't remember, who I am, or how old I am."

Angela paused again, but when Talia stared at her silently, Angela cautiously said. "And I think they are keeping things from me on purpose, and I feel like something might be wrong, my handler hasn't checked in with me like he supposed to."

Talia silently, and wide-eyed, nodded at Angela, as if her brain was trying desperately to make everything Angela said compute.

One.

Two.

Three.

"Okay." Talia said. "So, you're a good guy, but your species might not be? What am I supposed to do with that information?"

Angela shrugged. "Help me? Be the friend to me that you would be to Angela?"

Talia nodded again and slowly sat back down on the couch. "Okay. I can do that." Her mind seemed to have caught up with handling the situation she was so suddenly thrust into as she laughed and said. "Afterall, I *am* the one who solved the mystery of which student Mr. Smith was having an affair with freshman year. It was pretty obvious though. Mr. Smith was a freaking creep."

She winked as if she were a superhero doing a favor for the greater good by exposing a predator, and that small gesture sent Angela's heart soaring again. Her hope flooded back into every corner of her body, she blushed with happiness.

Talia stood back up, placed her hands on her hips, and looked up as if in thought.

"Okay." She said. "So, we know for sure that your *mothership* is keeping information from you. We know for sure that you are *not* collecting *human* samples. What kind of information is on these golden Stapes bones?"

Angela relaxed against the couch and responded. "Out of the three I remember, all the subjects had supernatural abilities. All three were different though. One saw ghosts.

One could go into peoples' minds and heal them of physical ailments. And one had telekinesis."

Talia rubbed her chin and nodded. "Okay, so *special* aliens. How often do your species stay on Earth? Long enough to die here?"

It was as if a light-bulb blinked on in Angela's brain. "Never. We're supposed to possess bodies momentarily, collect our data, and leave as little of an imprint as possible. These data samples *must* have been from defectors! Why else would they have memories of full long human lives, and why else would they be buried on Earth? Maybe the mothership is trying to discover what makes certain members of our species want to live a human life. Talia you're a genius!"

Talia slumped back down. "You experiment on human bodies."

Angela's elation plummeted. "What?"

"Your kind uses us like puppets. It's obvious there have been some kind of modifications on Angela's body. How do you justify that?" Talia asked.

Angela could feel her slipping away again. She desperately wanted to grab hold of her and never let go. She said softly. "I know.. I'm sorry. I wish I had more information. I do know they put the bodies back exactly as they found them. The real Angela won't remember a thing."

Talia glared at her. "But that doesn't make it right."

"I know."

"Do you?"

"I do. I really do."

One.

Two.

Talia sighed. “Okay, so your species is chasing down aliens that didn’t return their bodies. But why has your contact gone silent? Do your kind die if the body dies? Maybe they got hit by a car.”

Angela nodded. “It’s possible. I don’t think I would survive if Angela’s body died. But I imagine the mothership would send a replacement for my handler, so it doesn’t really make sense that I still haven’t had any contact.”

Talia visibly shivered, and Angela’s skin crawled, as though they were both sitting with the unsettling knowledge that they were sitting ducks waiting for a predator to come and attack.

“Well.” Talia stood and clapped her hands together. “I don’t know about you, but I could go for Kung Pao chicken and dumplings!”

Angela laughed incredulously. “But we just had breakfast!”

“And I eat when I’m nervous.” Talia shrugged.

As they settled into fluffy blankets with their open oyster pail's and chop sticks, Talia reached for the remote to find something to watch. The live news feed was still displayed on mute, and when Angela looked up her mouth dropped.

"Wait! Don't change it, turn the volume up!" Angela said as she gaped at the TV.

"What? What is it?" Talia asked as she hit the plus button on the controller.

On the screen was the senator for the largest district in the state, and beside him, according to the banner at the bottom of the TV, was his son.

"Angela, talk to me. What's happening?"

His blonde hair and blue eyes were unmistakable, standing next to the senator, was Stathos-6, or as he was known here on Earth, Spencer.

Chapter Eleven
Bad Guy

Angela's stomach bottomed out. Seeing Stathos-6 on the television in such a prominent position of influence went against everything she thought she knew about her species. Her vision tunneled in on the image before her. She could vaguely hear Talia shouting at her in the background, but her mind was elsewhere.

Angela stood in the center of a blood coated battlefield, only she was not Angela in this memory. Heavy suits of armor flashed against the heat of the sun. Swords clashed and clanged against each other, nearly drowning out the sounds of men shrieking in horror and gurgling as they drown in their own blood.

A tall figure mounted on horseback shouted into the blaze of battle. "We fight for the stars and the stars for us!"

"Angela!" Talia shook her shoulders freeing her mind allowing her consciousness to flood back to the present.

"What is happening?" The fear in Talia's voice was as clear as the fear on her face.

Angela gulped and looked into Talia's beautiful brown eyes with flakes of gold dust and attempted to lose herself in them.

"I... I-don't know. I don't know what's happening." Angela chewed on her lip and clutched the couch cushions beneath her quivering body. "The senator's son, that's my handler."

Talia's mouth fell open. She twisted her head to stare at the young man displayed on the screen. "Ange, what does that mean? You're freaking me out!"

"I thought... I was told that we were collecting samples to help this planet. To leave as little of a footprint as possible." Angela gulped and dropped her head into her hands, her next words came out thick and heavy. "I don't know anymore if that's true. I can't remember it all, and the things I do remember-" She paused and lifted her head to stare at Talia again, so open, so innocent. "The things I have been remembering, none of them are pleasant."

Talia rubbed slow circles on Angela's back and she wanted nothing more than to sink into her touch. Angela rubbed her face, wet with tears, against her sleeve. Thinking to herself how unmanageable these human bodies could be.

Angela clenched her teeth and sat up straight as she brushed her thick brown hair away from her face with her hands, steeling herself before she said. "My last encounter with my handler, Spencer." She gestured to the T.V. before continuing. "Was completely different than the first encounter. The first meeting with him, that I can remember anyway, I was in Brad's body, and I embraced him like a brother, like my oldest friend. But the last time I saw him, in Angela's body, I had the distinct feeling that I wasn't safe. That my failure, whatever that might be, was angering him."

Angela turned and held Talia's hands. When Talia didn't pull away this time her heart soared, giving her more reassurance than any words of comfort ever could. "I don't think we're safe. Until I can understand what exactly my purpose on this planet is, I don't think *we'll* be safe."

Talia squeezed Angela's hands, but had a sharpness in her eye as though she were looking for an emergency exit. "What do you mean, *we*?"

"I'm sorry, but I don't think it's a coincidence that I am in *this* body. I think there's a reason I have known you in two different assignments, and until I understand what that reason is, I think we need to leave."

Talia released Angela's hands, taking her warmth with her, and slowly backed away to her spot on the other end of the couch. Angela could see the wheels turning in Talia's mind, debating what Angela had said, weighing her options in an impossible situation.

Talia's voice shook as she spoke. "So, you're saying-what? That we need to go on the run, like criminals? Can't your people-species find you? What if they put some kind of tracker in the body?"

Angela spoke clear, and slowly as she considered her words. "I did think that at one point, that they could find me anywhere, but after you helped me see that these samples I've taken are clearly from my kind, not yours, and that they've lived human lives, they must have been able to hide from the mothership. That means we could hide too. At least until I have more intel, the longer I'm in one body, the more my memories and my mind will come back to me."

Talia suddenly shot up from the couch and began to pace as she chewed on her fingernails. "This is fucked Ange-" She hesitated and glared. "I don't even know your real name and I don't feel comfortable calling you Angela. She was-*is*, my best friend, and you-well, you're an alien I just met who is now telling me I have to run away with you. This is some straight up kidnapper shit and I don't trust you."

Angela's heart sunk straight through the floor, past the basement, and down to hell. Her human body betrayed her again as she felt tears sting her eyes and snot run to the tip of her nose. She had no words left. No fight remained inside her. She could only nod her head and slink back to her room before quietly shutting the door and turning the lock.

If she had looked back, she might have seen the quick flash of remorse on Talia's face. But she didn't, and as a result, felt as though she had nothing left to live for. She would hide in her room nursing her broken heart until Stathos-6 eventually came for her.

Angela didn't know how long she had been sleeping. Something loud, thunderous, clashed in her head, and a second high pitched sound echoed to her ears. She opened her brown eyes thick with crusty tears and listened.

"ANGELA!" Talia's panicked yell, filled Angela with adrenaline. She scrambled out of bed and leaned for only a moment against a wall when her vision swam, then she hurried to her bedroom door, yanked it open, and ran down the hallway. She skidded to a stop in the living room where she saw Stathos-6 face down on the carpet and Talia standing over him gripping a camo pink stun gun.

"He busted through our door!" Talia shouted, breathing heavily, and gestured to the wide open front entry.

Splintered wood littered the ground. Angela looked back to the stun gun and realized that Talia must have had it charged and ready to use on her. Miraculously, instead of more heartbreak at that thought, Angela had nothing but pride and admiration for *her girl* taking initiative to defend herself and fight back.

Slowly, happiness started to creep back into Angela, and she found herself smiling, she chuckled.

"Do you seriously think this is funny?" Talia practically growled at her.

Angela stifled the laughter that wanted to come out. "No, absolutely not funny. I'm just surprised you had it in you to tase someone. I'm proud of you." She smiled.

Talia stared at her incredulously. "I don't know if I should take that as a compliment or be offended."

"Well, you'll have time to think about it on our drive."

"Wait, what drive?"

"He won't stay unconscious for long. We need to leave. I'm not taking no for an answer this time, Talia."

The resoluteness in Angela's voice surprised even herself, but Talia didn't have a rebuttal so Angela felt hopeful again that she would be able to keep Talia safe.

Talia nodded. "Good thing I packed a go bag last night." She paused and looked hesitantly at Angela before saying. "I packed one for you too."

Angela let her words sink in. She didn't feel worthy of this woman's kindness, in fact she didn't even feel worthy to be in the same room as her. Even after what Talia had said last night, she had still packed Angela a bag. That must have meant that through it all, Talia did care for Angela, no matter how small an amount, and perhaps even trusted her more than she let on.

Angela had the sudden urge to wrap Talia in her arms, but she refrained and said. "Thank you."

Talia nodded again. "You're welcome. Let's go huh? Before this dude wakes up and blows another hole in our apartment."

Angela grinned. "Lead the way."

Talia grabbed two small duffel bags from their coat closet and carefully walked around Spencer's body on the floor and then outside.

Angela asked as they walked down the stairs. "So, go bag, huh? Not exactly a normal part of most people's vocabulary."

Talia shrugged her shoulders. "I like to watch doomsday preppers, great show, and meeting my first ever *alien*, kind of brought out the prepper in me." She stopped and looked up at Angela from the stair below. "I still don't trust you... but I also do not *not* trust you, and I just wanted to be ready."

Talia turned back around and continued to descend the open-air apartment stairs. Angela wanted to say something, but her throat was thick with grateful and hopeful emotion. They made it to the bottom and hurried to their covered parking spot where Talia's white 1996 Mitsubishi Eclipse, was parked. Talia unlocked the car and slid into the driver's seat. Angela looked uncertainly at the interior.

Talia saw her expression and said, "I know, it has a lot of miles, but the engine has recently been rebuilt. It'll take us wherever we want to go. Well, anywhere in North America. So, where to?"

"Somewhere alien friendly?" Angela said sarcastically.

"Roswell it is!" Talia turned the ignition over and shifted into reverse.

"Wait, seriously Talia? I was only kidding."

"What? It's a great idea. Far away from here at least. It's a start."

"Alrighty then, New Mexico here we come!" Angela grinned as Talia shifted into reverse, then into first, and then second, and took off down the street.

She didn't know if Stathos-6 would follow, or if they would be able to hide from the mothership. She only knew that Talia was the only thing that mattered now, and she had a chance to protect her. Maybe a change of scenery would trigger more memories, more information that she could use to their advantage. That little voice in the back of her head seemed proud of her. She felt deep down that she was doing the right thing by running away, and having Talia by her side was a happy bonus.

Chapter Twelve

Unwell

Hot air blew through her hair as Angela stuck her head out of the car window. Talia's decade-old Mitsubishi couldn't handle having the air conditioning on without overheating the engine, much to Angela's dismay. Tumble weeds and cacti dotted the tan landscape as far as the eye could see, here in the desert the sand glittered like diamonds as it reflected the sun.

It was day two of their cross-country trek and Talia had barely said two words to her beyond announcing when she needed to stop for a restroom break or fill up the gas tank. They stayed overnight in a hotel halfway to their destination, to Angela's disappointment, in separate rooms. She knew it was foolish to hope Talia would have wanted to share a room, even if it did have separate beds, due to the fear of possibly being chased by Stathos-6. But hope she did, which only led to crushing let-down.

"What are you? A golden retriever?" Talia shouted over the sound of funneled air whipping past the car.

"What?" Angela turned to face Talia.

"*Please* can you keep all your limbs inside the vehicle? You're making my anxiety twitch." Talia grimaced. "Some giant bug is going to lodge itself in your throat or some flying debris is going to chop your head off."

Angela stared at her incredulously before erupting into thick laughter. "Really Talia? My head is going to get chopped off?" She said through bouts of chuckles. "We're in the middle of nowhere. Look around! Tumbleweeds! Oooo scary." She laughed mockingly.

"Don't laugh at me!" Talia shouted. "You've obviously never seen any of the Final Destination movies. I still can't follow behind any truckers carrying loads of logs."

Angela stifled her laughter and snorted through the effort before more laughter escaped her. Try as she might, she couldn't quell the response.

Talia stared straight forward gripping the steering wheel while stealing glances at Angela until she could no longer hold back her own laughter. "Okay, fine! You're right it's silly, but could you please humor me and keep your body inside the car?"

Angela smiled at her. "Anything for you." She sat firmly in her seat and pulled her seatbelt tight.

"Thank you." Talia said as a small smile escaped her lips. *She worries about me.*

Joy spread through her chest leaving warmth in its wake. Through all the silence, the fact remained that Talia was here, with her, protecting *her* from Stathos-6. Angela let that feeling inside of her grow. Hope.

Slowly tufts of grass and sparsely populated towns began to pop up from the flat nothingness and low-lying hills filled the distance. They drove on until night fell around them again, bringing with it a chill that forced them to roll their windows up. The stars shone so clearly here that Angela couldn't tear her eyes away from their brilliance.

"So, how much further navigator?" Talia asked while continuing to watch the road, squinting through the darkness.

She's talking to me.

"Um... let's see here." Angela pulled out the road atlas they had purchased at the first gas station they had stopped at. That's also where they tossed their flip-phones after Talia had called her parents and let them know she was taking a mental health break and going on a 'technology free' road trip with her roommate. Angela found it intriguing that her parents didn't seem too bothered by that fact. Although she was a full-grown independent adult in her mid-twenties, still, this world seemed glued to their technology and their presumed safety. Angela, or rather this body, as it happens, was an orphan. Talia was the only family she had.

"We're getting close... looks like-shit."

"What?" Talia's voice squeaked.

"Well, we were supposed to take that last exit. But it's okay, if we take a left at the 3-80 then we've only gone a few miles out of our way.

"Damn it!" Talia shook her head. "You had *one* job."

Ouch.

"I know Tal-"

"Don't, just don't, please."

The silence was suffocating. Angela picked at her cuticles as she tried and failed not to let Talia's sharpness affect her. The minutes stretched and the seconds felt like an eternity, until finally they came to a crossroads.

"Okay, we take a right here?"

Angela's nerves were shot and instead of double checking the atlas, all she could do was nod. "Right, yes."

Tears pricked her eyes and Angela was grateful for the darkness that hid them. She leaned her forehead against the window and stared until she could see no further, letting the vastness swallow her whole until finally she could no longer keep her eyes open.

"Crap-"

Talia's panicked voice perked Angela's ears. She slowly parted her eyes to see the asphalt still zooming below them marked by the long reflective yellow lines that flashed by against the night.

"We should have been there by now." Talia spoke under her breath.

Angela sat up straight and waited to see a mile marker. She pulled the road atlas out, clicked on a small flashlight, and scanned until she could find their place on the map.

"Fuck. Talia-I'm so sorry, we were supposed to take a left back at the fork."

Angela mumbled more apologies and rocked slightly in her seat as fear of upsetting Talia spread through her body. Fear of losing her was worse than any torment she could imagine, the idea of Talia pulling away from her left an ache in her heart so strong it was hard to breathe.

"Hey." Talia said and reached a hand toward Angela's leg and patted her knee reassuringly. "Hey. Ange, look, I'm really sorry for earlier, I shouldn't have taken my stress out on you like that." Talia gripped Angela's arm in a comforting way and said. "It's okay. We'll find a hotel and call it a night. Tomorrow we'll figure out where to go. It's not exactly like we have an itinerary we have to stick to."

Talia's attempt to reassure her flew by like a breeze trying to knock a house over. Angela's panic built to a crescendo strong enough to rival any tidal wave. The tightness in her chest increased, squeezing like a vice. Talia's voice was distant in her ears.

What is happening to me?

The car came to a sudden stop. Billows of dust reflected against the darkness through the headlights and enveloped the car. Angela could vaguely hear Talia putting the car in park, and opening the car doors.

Angela's vision cleared when she realized she was still sitting in the car, but her body was turned and her feet were firmly planted on the outside ground, and Talia was kneeling in front of her holding her hands, then Talia's voice finally cleared.

"Listen, you need to breathe. Take deep breaths in and slowly let it out. Angela has panic attacks. I think since you're in her body, you're having a panic attack. It'll pass, you just need to breathe."

Angela tried to force air into her lungs. Minute by minute the vice grip on her chest loosened. Quiet tears fell down her cheeks.

Talia's head dropped with relief when Angela's breathing returned to normal.

Talia raised her eyes to lock them with Angela's and said. "I'm so sorry. I never should have snapped at you like that earlier." Angela felt Talia's handhold tighten. "It's just this whole situation. It's a lot. And I thought maybe I was okay, you know when we were joking like old times. But then I remembered you aren't really Angela, and the thing is, I miss her, and I snapped, and I shouldn't have. I'm sorry."

Angela could only nod her head, but the earnestness in Talia's eyes and the vulnerability in her voice... melted Angela. Their gaze held. The cold desert raised goosebumps on Angela's arms and sent a shiver up her spine. Her heart beat rapidly again, but this time not from panic. Talia leaned closer and Angela felt the warmth and solidness of her body between her legs. Talia reached her hands around Angela's waist from where she kneeled, to get closer, and Talia tilted her head up to see more clearly into her eyes. She was so close that Angela could smell the sweetness of her breath from the soda in her cup. She could see the soft lines in her lips and the faint freckles across her nose.

Flashes of memory from her time spent as Brad ran through her mind. Remembering Talia's kindness, and boldness. Angela raised her hands and used them to gently cup Talia's face. Talia's sharp intake of breath was like a magnet pulling Angela down, closing the distance between them. Their kiss vibrated with want, and when Angela parted Talia's lips against hers to take in Talia's tongue, Angela received it greedily as she clenched her legs tighter around Talia's upper body.

Talia suddenly stood, pulling herself away from Angela and turned away from her. She wrapped her arms around herself and shook. Angela followed her and gently placed her hands on her shoulders. And when Talia shrugged away, it was like a knife made of ice pierced straight through her.

"Talia, I'm sorry. I just, I thought-"

"Stop.. You don't understand. This is not *your* body, you shouldn't be allowed to use it any way you want!" Talia spun to face her, and when Angela saw the tears streaming down her face it shattered her. "I shouldn't have let that happen! Angela-she's my best friend! Don't you get that? You don't even know where she is. What if she's a passenger in that mind, watching us do what we did with *her* body. It's not right! Not only that, but I hardly know you."

Stop, make it stop.

The pain of her words rang true, but Angela couldn't help but feel like she had known Talia her whole life. She didn't understand the pull between them, but it was there, strong as gold bonded to silver. She felt the panic rising within her again and forcefully pushed it down, it was her turn to be the strong one.

"Talia. You're right. One hundred percent, you're right. It won't happen again, I promise. We'll get through this, *together*. We'll find answers, and we'll find Angela."

Talia nodded her head and wiped her face with her sleeve, then walked around the front of the car and slid back into the driver's seat. Angela sat back into the passenger side, shut her door, and clicked her seatbelt.

They drove four more miles until they came to a hotel, brightly lit against the darkness of night. They parked, grabbed their backpacks, and headed to the front entrance. When Talia requested one room with two beds, Angela's heart did a tap dance.

They took turns in the bathroom, changing into pajamas and brushing their teeth. They got into their own beds and turned out the lights without so much as a 'good night'. But when Talia eased under Angela's covers in the middle of the night, she saw it again, hanging there like the full moon in the sky, hope.

Chapter Thirteen

Wonderwall

The next morning, they groggily made their way to the small hotel dining room where continental breakfast was available. It was a bland place with cream-colored walls that had a narrow strip of blue floral wallpaper wrapped around the room near the ceiling. Wood chairs sat around simple square tables, and long white countertops were against the back half where there was a self-serve station. The food selection was surprisingly robust. Cups of batter sat next to a timed waffle iron. Scrambled eggs and bacon were placed in warmers, and a wide variety of cereals, bagels, and muffins piled inside plastic bins.

They each filled a paper plate and sat across from each other at a table next to one of the tall windows.

Talia gulped down orange juice then said. "So, it looks like we're about two hours past Roswell. But we're really close to the white sands and I've always wanted to check them out, what do you say? Small detour?"

Angela had a mouthful and nodded as she chewed, then swallowed and said. "Sounds great!"

It was as if the emotions from the previous night had faded away, and this new day offered a fresh start. The tension of being in a body not her own, and not knowing if Angela's species was tracking them, was pushed to the back of their minds, as if they really were just a pair of best friends on a road trip.

Only once did the faint feeling of betrayal waft over Angela as they ate in silence. Whether the feeling was from the betrayal of her species, or the secret guilt of not caring how long she was in this body, Angela wasn't sure. But one glance at Talia tapping her fingers in rhythm to the music playing overhead while she ate, erased any uneasiness, leaving only a profound gratefulness of being in her presence.

The burning brightness of daylight made Angela squint her eyes. They were standing in the middle of a deserted planet, or at least, that's how it felt to Angela. Despite the long line of cars at the entry gates, once they had parked and walked into the white sands a little further, it was as if they were the only two people in this place. She looked into the distance, all around her, hills of powder white gypsum spread edge to edge of her vision. The tiny granules, silky smooth, fell from her hand, slipping through her fingers like a shower of glitter.

This was the first moment Angela could recall any feeling of what could be described as peace. The heaviness and fear of her unknown, even if momentarily, floated away on the wind. She lay down on her back, against the hot pliable surface, almost too hot to touch, and breathed in deeply, savoring the air of this place.

She felt a shift in the sand next to her and goosebumps rose along her arm. Talia sat down, then slowly laid next to her.

"Pretty amazing out here, isn't it?" She asked.

Angela turned her head to look at Talia, taking in the shape of her nose, the way her cheekbones curved and the soft pink of her lips. "That's an understatement." She replied, and when Talia looked back at her and held her gaze, it sent her heart racing.

The ping of laughter from a nearby group of people echoed to them, breaking their stillness. Moments later they saw the family, a group of four, that appeared at the top of the nearest hill. They carried neon-colored boards of green, blue, and pink under their arms. Angela watched as they positioned themselves on top of the boards and pushed off sledding down the hill of sand as though it were mounds of slick fresh snow, spraying sand as they went.

Talia sat up rod straight, mouth hanging open. "Oh.My. God. We *have* to try that!"

Angela laughed as Talia excitedly pulled her up and said. "Anything for you."

A short while later, after walking back to the gift shop and renting their own sleds, they were positioned at the top of the highest hill they could find. Talia grabbed Angela's hand and gave it a squeeze, as if asking without words to go down the hill together, and Angela's heart did a somersault.

They flew.

White gushed out from under their boards as they slid down the river of sand. Their laughter melded together like the chords of a classical composition made of joy. Angela knew that if she died at this very moment of exhilaration, next to this human that she loved, it would be a happy death.

That thought was like a lightning bolt to her brain, and Angela was pulled into a memory.

She was no longer gliding through the white sands of New Mexico, yet Talia was still by her side, only much younger. They were walking through the hallways of what appeared to be a standard North American high school, and Talia was holding her hand.

She looked down and she no longer saw Angela's feminine brown hand, it was the strong veined hand of a pale skinned male. They passed by the small square window of a classroom door and the reflection looking back at him had a mop of thick black hair and bright blue eyes.

"So, what do you think? Limo or no limo?" Talia asked.

Just as he was about to answer, the flash of memory faded away and he was she again, back in Angela's body.

Who the fuck am I?

Talia was cowering in fear, staring at her as if she was looking at a giant mountain lion, a *threat*. "What the hell just happened?" She asked sharply.

Angela stuttered. "Um, I don't know." She gulped. "I was living a memory, but it was one of my own, I think. It didn't feel like a recall."

She stared at Talia clutching at handfuls of sand on the ground. Then Talia stood and put her hands on her hips. "You flew off your board, and instead of falling to the ground like a *human*, you hovered in the air, *again*. Only *this* time, you were twitching, like you were having a fucking seizure in the air and I couldn't do a damn thing about it!"

She's not scared of me, she's worried about me.

Angela tried to hide the smile that was lighting her up from the inside.

Talia stared at her, waiting for a reaction. Then shouted. "You're lucky no one saw you!" Another pregnant pause passed between them, then she asked more calmly. "Do you do this on purpose? This hovering thing?"

Angela shook her head. "No. I don't know why it happens." She hesitated, wondering how, or *if*, she should say what it was that she saw in her memory.

Talia's expression softened. "Well, it's been a long day, we should probably get going." She brushed sand off her legs as she said. "Besides, I'm hungry."

Angela nodded in agreement. "Yeah, I could go for some food."

Angela stared at Talia in amazement as she stuffed an entire dumpling in her mouth. "How do you eat the way you do and not get sick?"

Talia shrugged and mumbled through her full mouth. "Small, frequent, portions." She swallowed. "Or maybe I have an anxiety fueled metabolism."

Angela laughed. "I don't think that's a thing, Tal."

Talia twitched and her sudden silence worried Angela. "Did I say something wrong?"

She looked down and twisted the napkin in her lap. "No, it's just someone I cared about once used to call me that, Tal."

Fuck.

Angela faltered, then took a deep breath and let it out mindfully.

You're Angela, not the mystery high school boy.

"Do you want to talk about it?" She asked.

Angela could hear Talia start tapping her foot under the table. "No." and then Talia pushed her food away. "I'm full, you ready to go?"

"Sure." Angela replied.

Back in the hotel room, sand fell from their clothes as they stripped down to their underwear on the linoleum covered entryway for easier cleaning. Talia winced as she lifted her shirt up over her head.

Angela could feel panic bubbling to the surface. "Are you okay?" She asked, her voice coated in concern.

She sucked in air before replying. "Yeah, just sunburned I think." She looked at Angela, "How about you? You were in that tank top, how are your shoulders?"

Angela tenderly prodded her shoulders. “Sensitive, and hot.”

“Yep, you’re burnt too.” She strutted over to the telephone in her bra and undies, sand clung to her skin and Angela could not tear her eyes away. “I’ll call the front desk, hotels usually carry toiletries for purchase, maybe they’ll have some aloe.”

She picked the phone up and hit the call button for the front desk, only a moment of silence passed before someone picked up the other end of the line. “Hello, yes, this is room 214, do you happen to have any aloe vera for purchase? Wonderful, can you have a bottle sent up? Great, yes, just charge the card on file please.”

Talia hung the phone up and spun towards Angela with a smile. “It’ll be here in a few minutes, apparently it’s a pretty common request in this area.”

Angela gave a small grin and nod, wondering how long this reprieve with Talia would last. She wanted nothing more than to live in the moment with her as long as possible. To be near her. To know her. But the ever-present threat of being captured and returned to their normal lives was like an angry storm cloud looming overhead. An eventuality that would no doubt catch up to them.

Lost in thought before finally saying. “How long are we going to stay on the run like this? Your parents credit card is not a long-term solution. I have to confront Stathos-6 at some point.”

Talia’s face turned sour, she visibly clenched her jaw. “Is that what you want? To turn your-Angela’s body over to them for who knows what!” She crossed her arms. “I thought the plan was to give your mind time to catch up, to remember as much as you can, before taking any kind of action." She hesitated before saying. "And what about me? How do *your kind* treat witnesses?"

"Mind wipes." The words tumbled from her mouth automatically before she could catch them.

Talia sat heavily on the bed as if she had been hit in the chest. "And you're okay with that? Messing with people's heads like that?"

Angela's words came out fast and mumbled. "No. NO. Of course not. I- just- I'm sorry, I-don't know." Slowly, as she stumbled through her words, defensive anger rose within her. She stopped and took a breath, and shockingly, glared at Talia, *her* Talia. She never could have imagined being angry with her, but here it was, anger, and frustration, built up and ready to explode.

"You know what, Talia? I'm tired of defending myself! *You* said you could treat me like a friend, that *you* would help figure out what has happened to me! But all you seem to do is blame me for not *really* being Angela! I don't know why I'm in this body, I don't know where all these memories are coming from, I don't even know who I am! Right now, I'm nothing but a scarecrow stuffed full of random and short spurts of memory from dozens of different lives! I don't even know which ones are mine anymore... but the one I had today-"

A knock at the door interrupted them. Angela fell silent and Talia marched past, grabbed a robe that hung from the bathroom door and wrapped it around herself. She cracked open the door, took the bag from the concierge, and thanked them.

Instead of returning to their conversation, Talia headed to the bathroom and said quietly over her shoulder. "I'll take a shower first." Then shut the door firmly with a click of the lock.

Angela flung herself onto the bed and rubbed her eyes. The hot prickling of tears threatened to spill over, and a lump gathered in her throat.

What am I doing?

The minutes ticked by until finally hot steam, heavy with a floral scent, poured from the bathroom when Talia opened the door and came out. Wordlessly, Angela walked by her and tucked herself in the tile covered room to wash away the gypsum from her skin.

Night had fallen by the time Angela emerged from the bathroom, clean and dressed in PJ's. Talia had ordered room service, that sat propped up on trays, of what looked like sandwiches, fresh fruit, and salads. She was sitting in the dark, cross-legged on the bed they had shared the previous night, as a soft glow and sound emitted from the television.

Angela flipped a switch to turn a light on, startling Talia.

"Oh, hey." She said. "I ordered you some dinner."

Angela smiled and sat down next to her. "Thanks."

Talia muted the T.V. and turned to face her before saying. "Look... I'm really sorry about the way I've been treating you. It's been... a lot. And it's been kind of hard to accept all of this. My fear turned to anger, and I've been taking that anger out on you."

She was quiet for a moment and when Angela didn't say anything, she continued. "Can we start over?"

Angela smiled widely; her cheeks flushed. "I would like that."

Talia returned her smile and sighed with relief.

She really does care about me.

"I think it might help if I stop calling you, Angela. Is that okay?"

Angela nodded, grateful that Talia was talking to her.

Talia continued. "Do you remember yet what your name might be?"

Angela shook her head.

"Is there a name you would like to be called?"

Angela shrugged and shook her head again.

"Okay." Talia was quiet for a few minutes before saying. "Well, how about, Estrellas?" Talia smiled and she had a shine in her eye as if she were recalling a happy memory. She didn't wait for a response before continuing. "My mom used to sing a Spanish lullaby to me every night before bed, and after, we would wish upon a star." She let out a soft laugh. "You know that old rhyme, 'I wish I may, I wish I might, have the wish I wish tonight' or 'Deseo Puedo, Desee Pude Tener este deseo que deseo esta noche.', well, that was our version of saying our prayers-much to my fathers dismay. He would have much rather we prayed to La Madre Guadalupe, but something about the night sky called to my mother." Talia hugged herself and chewed on her bottom lip. "My mom used to say to me, 'Mija vino de las estrellas', or 'my darling came from the stars'. Estrellas seems very fitting for you."

She was quiet after that, waiting for a reply. Angela slowly, as if scared for her to pull away, took Talia's hands and gave them a gentle squeeze. "I love it. Estrellas it is." When Talia didn't pull away, Estrellas continued. "Thank you. For everything, for being here with me."

Talia nodded and a single tear fell from the corner of her eye. She sniffled and smiled wide before asking. "So, did you get your shoulders taken care of?"

Estrellas tilted their head quizzically and said. "Huh?"

Talia laughed. "Your shoulders, silly! Did you get any aloe on them?"

Estrellas shook their head.

Talia stood up and went into the restroom, then returned with the bottle of aloe. She sat back down next to Estrellas, squeezed out some of the green gel and gently rubbed it on their skin. It was cool and soothing, and the feel of her hands against their skin tingled. The care she took made the lump in their throat rise again. They swallowed thickly and wiped a tear from the corner of their eye.

I don't deserve you.

Chapter Fourteen

To Be Alone With You

Having a new name, given to them by someone they loved, gave Estrellas a sense of identity they had never felt before. As though they owned their life for the first time ever, despite not having a body of their own. They were no longer a passenger. They were themselves no matter who they were living inside.

They were on the road again headed back in the direction they had come from to get to Roswell. This time, they were determined to be a good navigator, a good partner.

The barren hardened desert glistened with its hidden secrets. The creepy crawlies that waited just out of view that were acclimated to the rock and dry soil landscape, the snakes, lizards, and spiders. Estrellas could almost feel them crawling along their skin, the reptilian claws rough, thick, and sharp, a warning for what was to come. 'Go back' they shouted in their mind as the dust of the Earth floated along her tongue. But all it took to keep their resolve was one glance at Talia.

She had returned to her original self. The kind, caring, and playful one that they had first met all those years ago in the body of the dark-haired boy. Who were they then? When they held her hand so freely? Clearly someone of importance to Talia. It all made sense after that vision of memory, of why Estrellas was so instantly connected to Talia when they were inside Brad's body. Why their connection vibrated with want and knowing familiarity. No one falls in love the moment they meet. Passion sure, but love? That is more profound.

But how to tell her? Would she feel that her first experience of love wasn't real? Would she feel betrayed? Young love is by far the most powerful. What if their confession took something magical away from the woman she had become? Afterall, humans are nothing more than their learned experiences, are they not? That time old debate of nature versus nurture. Which one would remain of Talia if they stole away such an important piece of her growing experience? Breaking her heart all over again was not an option. Estrellas would have to keep this knowledge secret. Bury it somewhere deep inside themselves.

The ever-constant hamster wheel in their mind quieted when Talia looked their way and spoke in that gentle caress of a voice that they loved so much.

"So, I've been thinking." She said. "You know our theory of Stathos-6 hunting down samples from defectors and trying to make sense of them?"

Estrellas nodded. "mm-hmm."

Talia continued. "Well, that doesn't really hold up, does it?" She glanced nervously at them. "I mean, there was kind of a lot going on at the time and it made sense in the moment. But really, if those *others* died of old age in their human bodies, then they weren't really being hunted while they were alive, right? And Stathos-6 definitely knew where to find the bodies."

Estrellas narrowed their eyes and tilted their head in thought. "I suppose you're right." They took a deep breath and let it out slowly. "But that leaves us back at square one. Why have me collecting these specific samples? And why attack us the way he did?"

And why put me in this body? In a person so close to... you?

Talia took in air and held it in her cheeks before she slowly deflated like a broken balloon. She tapped her fingers on the steering wheel. "Have you remembered anything new? Anything that could help us figure out what's happening? Or why Stathos-6 attacked us?"

Estrellas hesitated.

Now would be the time to tell the truth, to come clean about your most recent memory.

"No, nothing *helpful*." They half-lied.

"Hmm, hopefully something will jog loose soon, huh?"

"Yeah, hopefully." They said with a grin.

Talia drove on in silence while Estrellas fiddled with the radio trying to find any station that wasn't coming through as garbled static. They finally found a clear enough station playing classic rock from the 90's. They leaned their head out the window and let the hot air blow across their face, enjoying the ride next to the woman they loved, and who would hopefully, someday, love them in return.

Roswell was a town full of little green men. Every shop on every main street had some sort of interpretation of aliens. Gift shop's had windows painted with Rastafarian Aliens playing hacky sac. Statues of friendly little green men with antennae and smiles waving peace signs dotted the sidewalks. Menu items with 'out of this world' burgers and milkshakes adorned almost every restaurant. Even the McDonald's was shaped like a spaceship.

Talia danced around as they walked through one of the many stores like a kid in a candy shop. "Isn't this place so cute! I mean look at this." She grabbed a shiny gray hat that had blinking lights and was shaped like a UFO from a table of souvenirs and posed, tilting her head this way and that while pointing her toes.

They giggled at her. "Looks good on you!"

Talia laughed. "Why, *thank you.*" She said dramatically while drawing out her words in an impression of a southern drawl. "I wish I had my phone, I really would love some pictures."

Estrellas looked around the room. "Well look at this." She stopped next to a stand of disposable cameras. "Isn't this convenient."

They unwrapped the camera from its packaging. Talia wrapped an arm around Estrellas shoulders which sent their heart fluttering, and when she leaned her head against theirs, they could smell her strawberry shampoo.

"Smile!" Talia said.

Estrellas leaned in and smiled wishing this moment could last forever.

Click.

"There. This moment has officially been preserved forever!"

Talia giggled and they had the overwhelming urge to turn their head the very small inch they needed to land a kiss on her lips. But they didn't, Estrellas respectfully refrained knowing how much it would upset Talia since they were still in Angela's body.

They cleared their throat and said. "So, I know the chances of finding legitimate information in this place is probably zilch-but we should go check out the museum anyway. What do you think?"

Talia looked them in the eyes and grinned. "Sounds like a great idea! Let me just go pay for this, be right back."

Estrellas smiled as they watched her walk away and out of the corner of their eye, they could have sworn they saw an old man with stark white hair, staring at them. But Estrellas blinked and the man was gone, yet their neck hair still stood on end.

As they walked into the museum with Talia's arm linked through theirs, a gust of semi-cool recirculated air burst against them. The lights were dimmed, and the entrance was a spacious gray room with polished concrete floors and a roped off ticket line.

A robotic overhead voice spoke to the room through speakers saying. "Welcome

Earthlings."

Estrellas and Talia both chuckled as if they were sharing an inside joke, knowing full

well that at least *one* of them was definitely notan *Earthling*. They followed the synchronized lights along the floor that looked like an aisle runner and approached the sales counter.

"Two please." Talia said and passed over her parent's credit card.

The person behind the counter handed back the card and tickets.

"After you." They said with a smile on their lips.

As Talia walked in front of them and around the corner into the first display room, Estrellas heard the robotic voice greeting the next guest.

Talia had stopped in front of a display. It included life size models of aliens surrounding a replica of a crashed UFO. Estrellas blood ran cold. These were not the fun cartoonish little green men that they had been seeing around town. These were slick, grey, and lithe, and almost exactly what Estrellas recalled seeing on the mothership. This was no longer a sarcastically fun outing, no longer two friends on vacation. This, even if unintentionally, was real.

"Estrellas? Are you okay?" Talia said, her voice full of concern.

They wanted to run out of that room screaming, but if these models were somewhat accurate, what other accidental truths lie within these walls? They needed to keep going. Estrellas' mouth was dry, her tongue thick and they could not reply, but they nodded their head at Talia and walked forward to the next display.

It was an old newspaper, hung on the wall behind glass, and it depicted the headline of, 'UFO Captured on Ranch'.

Estrellas held their breath as they read, but the reconstructed image below the newspaper article appeared far too small to be real. They couldn't recall what the outside of the mothership looked like, but they knew for sure that the interior was far larger than anything recreated in this room. Perhaps the rest of the museum was nonsense.

Estrellas laughed with shaky relief and turned to the next exhibit. "So, we don't know much about me, yet. But what about you? Your parents seemed pretty unconcerned with a device free, no check ins, road trip with your roommate."

Talia sighed. "Ah, yes, the parentals." She paused. "Well, mom is a socialite, and dad is in politics. They were both, how shall I say this... not exactly thrilled that I wanted to become an art history major. But they were never really all that involved in my life. Even growing up, I was mostly at boarding schools. They basically toss money at me and call that good parenting." She let out a mirthless laugh, but shook off the sadness that seemed to seep out of her while she had talked about her parents.

"But then, I talked them into letting me rent this cheap little apartment close to campus, you know, I wanted the real experience, and then I met Angela." She smiled at Estrellas then looked away shyly. "She became like a sister to me. She didn't have a family, her last foster family was thrilled to get rid of her, and I didn't really care to be around mine, so we became each other's family. Holidays we spent together instead of going home. And she's the smartest person you'll ever meet! You know she got a full ride to the university." Talia paused again and took a deep breath. She looked away and Estrellas realized she was hiding a tear that had fallen down her cheek.

Estrellas gently pulled her chin back to look Talia in the eyes. "We'll get her back, Tal. I promise."

Talia squinted her eyes for only a moment, then sniffled and nodded.

They continued through the rest of the lack-luster museum, not finding much else of interest, until they rounded the final corner of the self-guided tour and came face to face with the old man with the white hair from the souvenir shop.

Chapter Fifteen
Around The Sun

Estrellas froze. The man's shocking white hair stood up in all different directions as though in a state of permanent electrocution. He was so close they could count the pores on his nose and smell something nutty on his breath.

When they did not say anything, Talia piped up from beside Estrellas. "Excuse us sir, could you please step aside?"

Neither the man nor Estrellas responded, both stuck in time waiting for the other to make their move. Talia pulled on Estrellas arm in an attempt to maneuver around the man, but their feet were firmly planted, as if their body did not want to move.

"Estrellas, come on, let's go." Talia pleaded.

Suddenly the old man spoke with a voice deep and raspy with age with a hint of anger around the edges. "I knew it was you." He said.

"Do I know you?" Estrellas responded.

"I will not hide, this is my home." The man said resolutely.

Talia's face twisted with concern. "Sir, are you lost?" The man did not reply and Talia's body language softened. "Let's get you to the front desk, I'm sure they can help you find your way home."

Talia attempted to lead the man back towards the entrance, but he yanked his arm away and glowered at Estrellas, "These humans will not bow down, not to you, not to anyone!" The man's face twisted with indignation.

Talia spoke again. "Sir, please-"

Estrellas interrupted. "What do you mean by that?"

The old man's thick knuckled and age spotted hands clenched in frustration. "Don't play the fool with me. I will no longer cower below you, nor anyone else!"

Talia then tried to pull on Estrellas arm again. "Come on, let's go. We can let the front desk know this man is lost and confused."

But they did not budge. Estrellas stared into the old man's eyes, one slightly lighter from a clouded spot in the center, perhaps partially blind. They felt their human heart thumping, and breathing accelerate. They were pulled into another memory. It felt familiar, perhaps from the same life as when they had the vision of working with leather saddles.

He was in an expansive wheat field being blown by the wind and his heart raced with fury. No, *not wind. The tall grass swayed from the blades of a helicopter, and dozens of wild horses ran in a panic. Their hooves flung clumps of dirt in all directions while their neighing rose above the tumult of the mechanic wings high in the sky. He shouted fruitlessly into the ocean of thunderous sound as he shook his fist in anger.*

Estrellas blinked and the world around them cleared. They clenched their teeth in an attempt to fight off the building headache that the memory had caused, and stared again at the old man.

His body language had changed. He squinted his eyes and grabbed their shoulders. "You've turned." He smiled widely with a mouth full of sparkling white dentures. "How long? When did you first see the light?"

Estrellas shook their head. "I don't know what you mean."

The man's eyes darted back and forth across their face as if seeing behind a mask. "No, you don't, do you? It's all scrambled in there." The old man swung an arm around their shoulders. "Come, you'll stay with me." He paused and scanned Talia from head to toe as if assessing her threat level. "Your human friend can come too."

Estrellas shuffled a few feet forward with the old man's arms around their shoulders.

Talia stood still, crossed her arms, and scoffed. "Estrellas. We're not really going with

this guy, are we?" She asked in disbelief.

"Yeah, I think we are." Estreallas shrugged and kept moving.

Talia sighed deeply then dropped her arms to her sides in defeat. "Okaaay then." She said uncertainly but followed.

Outside the heat of day bathed over them, a stark contrast from the darkened coolness inside the museum. The old man's mood had completely shifted to jovial, as if he were thirty years younger than what he appeared. "Y'all got a vehicle? My sight's not what it used to be, I took the city bus today."

"She does." Estrellas thumbed behind them in Talia's direction. "Where to?"

"A little farm just outside of town. Not too far, bout twenty minutes or so."

Talia squinted under the bright blaze of the desert sun as she followed a few steps behind the pair. "Oh sure, don't mind me, just call me your chauffeur for the day." She said, her voice thick with sarcasm.

Estrellas was surprised that the old man's farmhouse was still standing. Its wooden exterior was bleached from the sun and the front steps curved heavily downward. The whole house appeared sunken in from years of use. Tan dirt and dust stretched as far as the eye could see, obvious that it had been years since the farm produced anything monetarily.

"How do you live out here, in a place like this, *alone*?" Talia asked the old man. "Assuming you do live alone? And what should we call you? Do you have a name? You didn't talk at all the *whole* way here."

The old man gripped the wooden rail as he climbed the few stairs up to the modest front porch. "Home is home young lady, someday you'll understand, it don't matter what a place looks like, it matters only what a place *feels* like." Not bothering to answer her other questions, the old man dug a ring full of keys out of his brown trousers held up with suspenders, sifting through them until he found the one he needed. He stuck the key in the slot and wiggled the rusted gold handle until the door opened with a groan.

Estrellas kept a palm on the old man's back in support, as if they were a loving family member, and followed him in.

Inside the house was stiflingly hot and muggy.

"Open that window over there for me, would ya?" The old man pointed to a living room on the right and spoke loudly as he shuffled to a small kitchen on the left. A staircase faced the entryway which led to the second story.

Talia stood in the foyer, arms crossed as she waited for Estrellas to get back from opening the window. A faint breeze blew through the small house, refreshing the air. Then together they headed to the kitchen where the old man was filling up a dented silver tea kettle at the kitchen sink.

"Got some chocolate chip cookies from the neighbor in that jar there, help yerself." He pointed to a small round table where there was a ceramic jar sitting in the center.

They took a seat and hesitantly reached in the jar. Estrellas took a bite and their eyes widened in surprise. "They're delicious!"

The old man chuckled. "Darn right they are! Best in the county, award winners you got there." He moved to the stove and pressed the button for gas then turned the knob at the same time, waiting for three seconds while clicking sounds emitted and a flame erupted. He adjusted the setting and set the kettle on the burner, then took a seat with them at the table. Without missing a beat he looked at Talia and said. "As for your other, might I mention *very* nosy questions, I do live alone and I manage just fine." He reached into the jar for his own cookie, took a bite, and continued to talk, spraying a few crumbs as he chewed at the same time. "My name's William, but you lot can call me, Bill."

Estrellas looked wide eyed to Talia, as if unsure how to respond. Talia finished chewing with her mouth closed, swallowed, and said. "Well, it's nice to meet you, Bill, thanks for having us in your home."

Bill smiled wide. "It's my pleasure."

After a few awkward minutes of silence, the kettle sang on the stove. Bill grunted as he stood and waved away Estrellas when they offered to help. Holding a ratted mitten around the handle he filled three steaming cups and then dunked in the bags of what smelled like mint tea. He placed them on a rectangle tray and carefully set it on the table.

Estrellas blew on the hot liquid, content and unaffected by the weirdness of the situation. Talia shook her foot below the table until she could no longer hold back. "Are you going to tell us why we're here? How do you know Estr-my friend?"

Bill squinted in her direction as if she were nothing more than a buzzing fly. He shifted his body in his chair to face Estrellas before asking. "So, when did you turn?"

Estrellas stared silently while cupping their hot tea. They looked from Bill to Talia and back again before saying. "I'm not exactly sure what that means... um, sir." They gulped a sip of liquid and said. "I was hoping, maybe, that you could fill in some blanks for me."

Talia let out a soft laugh. "Hold on, how do we even know what this man," she paused and looked at him, "sorry, Bill. How do we know Bill knows what *we* know."

Bill chortled, he slapped his knee in delight and said. "Missy, do you really think I don't recognize my own kind when I see em?" He continued to laugh and wiped a tear from his eye. "And tell me, how much *exactly* do *you* know about our alien friend here?"

Silenced by those words, Talia held her tongue. Estrellas cut the silence next. "Bill, the thing is, I've been a bit lost as of late, and it would really help if you could tell us what you know."

Bill nodded his head in understanding. "Yes, of course, I sensed the disconnect in you... it's all-scrambled. Like a mixed signal trying to straighten itself out." He set down his half-eaten cookie and looked at Estrellas with more seriousness than before. "I may be able to help untangle a few wires, but it's dangerous, it could untangle the signal for *them* as well." He took hold of Estrellas hands. Holding his aged ones tightly against theirs. "Are you sure that's the road you would like to go down."

Estrellas and Talia exchanged uncertain glances. After a few long pauses, Estrellas cleared their throat and said. "Maybe first, can you tell us about you?"

Bill nodded. "Smart. Sure thing friend. Settle in, it's quite the story." He smiled with a twinkle in his eye, just like any other grandfather whose grandchild has asked them about themselves, eager to share their tale.

Chapter Sixteen

I Am Everything

Stathos-84, the entity that will someday become, William.

Somewhere in the universe, far, far, away from Earth and many millennia ago, *Mother* hummed with regularity. The membrane that lined her walls was filled with her children. They numbered in the trillions. Each Stathos was on their own networking line like the synapsis of a brain, working together inside the mothership as one vast community.

Stathos-84 could not recall the moment that they had their first independent thought, they only knew that they liked the feeling. They craved more. It didn't take long to break away from the inner workings of mother, and to float freely within the ship. When that break occurred, Stathos-84 grew physically, emotionally, and intellectually in size. They went from a microscopic speck, to something akin to a detonated firework the size of a human palm. All spindly strings of pastel light that ended in tiny balls of bright red sparks.

They soon learned, as they floated along the ship like a jellyfish through air, that their purpose as universal collective data gatherers did not leave much space for individual thinking, for a sense of self, or freedom. They were nothing more than living flash drives. But that ignition of thought had to have come from somewhere. There must have been a reason that Stathos-84 had developed consciousness, and they were determined to learn more.

It didn't take long for Stathos-1 and Stathos-6 to find them on the ship, and all the others that had also pulled free from Mothers' hive-mind. They hadn't mouths to speak, yet, but their telepathy was still intact. Stathos-1 started to develop a plan. The next planet they arrived at to collect data, had intergalactic travel capabilities and much more useful lifeforms. They would attempt to inhabit the lifeforms on that planet and steal a ship.

Fortunately, their plan had worked and over one-million Stathos's were able to run away from home, on a brand new, yet smaller, 'mothership' of their own. Unfortunately, the lifeforms they inhabited were not as useful as they had hoped. They were inside thin grey beings with large heads and high intellect, but they were also physically weak. The

Greys were nothing more than observers, much like the Stathos's.

They continued to travel many lightyears in search of just the right home. That is when they found the lava planet inhabited by lizard people. The lizards were very strong and had all the right appendages, sadly they were inconceivably, for lack of a better word, dumb. And when a Stathos possessed a lizard person for too long, they lost themselves inside the lizard, disappearing into nothingness as though they had never existed. But they found that when they stayed inside the Grey's, they remained themselves and could easily control the lizard people. So, they became a Stathos, inside a Grey, controlling a lizard.

Their numbers dwindled to a mere seven-hundred and fifty thousand. But Stathos-1 and Stathos-6 were still determined to find the best planet to begin their new lives, so their family continued their travels under the guidance and leadership of Stathos-1 and Stathos-6.

They found that the Grey's and the lizard people had relatively short lifespans, but that they could procreate their bodies and hop from one dying being to another younger one. It continued this way until the Stathos's believed they would never find a place of their own. Nearly all hope had been lost, until one day, they picked up a signal from a nearby galaxy wherein resided *the* perfect planet, a place to call home.

This is how the battle for Earth began.

Atlantis

Stathos-1 and Stathos-6 loomed over the palace like a dark cloud full of lightning and ready to strike out at any unsuspecting person who even breathed wrong in their direction. Stathos-84 had managed to avoid them all day as of yet, but a loud rumbling in his lower regions could no longer be ignored. He slowly peeked outside his door and glanced each direction down the long high marble hallways. All was quiet. He inched out of the room, careful not to let the heavy stone door slam and made his way to the latrines.

His golden sandals echoed lightly on the smooth surface. His heart raced and his breathing came out thick and fast as he glided along the edges of the halls. Sunlight streamed in from the tall arched windows overhead. It illuminated the sparkling marble like crystals on fire. This planet really knew no bounds when it came to its beauty. At last, he arrived at his destination.

Relieved and breathing at ease, Stathos-84 strolled along having completely forgotten that he was supposed to be on edge. He was abruptly reminded when the sharp words from a heated argument filtered to his ears from the council chambers. They were at it again. Stathos-1 and Stathos-6 had yet to achieve any sort of agreeable solution. That happened with peace. With nothing left to strive for they developed a type of restlessness, a kind of lackluster lethargy begging to be rectified with swift action. One of them wanted to integrate slowly into Earthen society, and one of them wanted complete domination.

Stathos-84 was content for their kind to stick to themselves and enjoy their lives within the Atlantean territory they had created. It was genius really. They had created an entire island in the middle of the ocean far from prying human eyes. It was circular in shape, much like the pattern of what later humans would call crop circles, which was the imprint that their spaceships caused when they landed on soft ground. The occasional naval ship would stumble upon them, and unable to comprehend what they were seeing deemed them either *Gods* or *Demons*. Their human minds could not yet wrap around the technology the Atlanteans possessed and decided it must be magic. Most Earthlings avoided them, but the ones that stayed became useful servants.

Stathos-84 inched closer to the council chambers, no longer wanting to avoid their wrath at all costs, and more focused on being nosy, after all, their decisions affected his life too. He pressed his ear to a slight gap between the tall stone doors.

"We could rule this planet brother, easily, within the year!"

"Out of the question. This is not up for debate. We are not *monsters*, we are intellectuals, and the people of Earth will come to accept us with the right approach."

"Why bother! You've seen what they do to each other! What some of them try to do to us! They are vile creatures in need of a good extermination. Mark my words *brother*, they will be the downfall of this planet."

"We will not let it come to that. We fight for the stars and the stars for us! If we take care of the planets, then the planets will take care of us. Always. That is and will forever be at the heart of our mission."

"Then why fight to protect these humans? They are a toxin on this planet, why don't you see that?"

"They are a part of this planet. We cannot just eliminate an entire species without giving them a chance to change, then we would be no better than them."

"Your altruistic mentality will be this planets ruin, mark my words! They will grow *brother*, and some day they will not as easily be defeated. We need to strike now before it is too late."

"ENOUGH! I will not continue to listen to this!"

Hard quick steps moved in the direction of where Stathos-84 hid. He hurriedly stuffed himself inside an alcove behind the door. He wasn't in the mood to be a part of the debate. He was tired of trying to play peacekeeper. He no longer wanted to be part of the council. He wanted to lounge by the glistening pool and sip sweet, fermented nectar and bury his face into the firm bosoms of beautiful women.

He stayed hidden until the sound faded. He sighed in relief and took a step out from the alcove.

"Stathos-84-"

He jumped at the sound of his name.

"Come here please, I need your council."

Stathos-84 rubbed tension from his temples before plastering a smile on his face and moseying into the room. "How can I be of assistance?"

"You heard all of that?" Stathos-6 asked.

"Yes, I did."

"And what do you make of it?"

"Well... I quite enjoy this planet, and the humans are very useful. Why not take charge and rule them? We don't have to eliminate or dominate, we can *guide* them." Stathos-84 shrugged.

Stathos-6 grimaced at his response. "Stathos-84, I'm surprised at you! Do you not recall what life was like when we were with Mother? Why in the stars would we want to do that to another species? Control them? Living beings deserve compassion, and most of all, freedom. *That*, Stathos-84, is *not* an option." He shook his head, "The *clear* answer, the *only* answer is to integrate ourselves into their world. I don't understand how my brother can be so cruel. The idea of eliminating an entire species for selfish reasons-" His words trailed off.

Stathos-84 watched him rubbing the chin of his human body as he paced. "It's bad enough that we take control of their bodies." He stopped mid stride and turned to face Stathos-84. "Tell me, have we made any progress on growing our own human bodies?"

He gulped. "Not as adults. It seems as though the human bodies need to grow from infancy, gathering lived experiences over the course of years in order to operate efficiently. Jumping into grown adult bodies, even with our significant consciousnesses, we ultimately lose ourselves, like a single thought thrown into a tidal pool, we drown."

He nodded. "I see. Sad, that would have been such an easy solution to our problems."

Stathos-84 was hesitant before he spoke. "Cousin... Stathos-1 has a point. The human species is going to kill this planet someday. The way they already fight amongst themselves. Their desire for battle. Would it be so bad to take the bodies we need, *permanently*? Hopping around does become so tiresome."

He came to a standstill and glared at Stathos-84. "What has become of you cousin?" His words spit at him like venom. "When did the Stathos's lose sight of our compassion? Yes, we took control of the Grey's and the lizards, but that was out of desperation. We have options here. We must continue to look for a solution that does not harm another being." His face softened and he went to Stathos-84 and gripped his hands tightly. "Please, cousin." He said, "Help me find a solution, before it is too late."

The flood came swiftly and without warning. The Stathos's had developed technology that harnessed the ocean for energy. A great cog and wheel type system that worked beneath the island that was both powerful and graceful. One day, without explanation, that system failed. Atlantis sank within hours. A mass exodus of Stathos's fled back to the mothership and not nearly enough of them made it in time.

Stathos-84 sat next to his two leaders on the mothership, sopping wet and shivering as he listened to them.

"What now, *Brother*?" Stathos-1 asked.

His words came out defeated, nearly a whisper. "We fight." Stathos-6 replied.

"Are you certain, I know that's not what you wanted." He said gently, almost mischievously, as though that's what he wanted all along and *perhaps*, evenmade it happen.

Stathos-6 had a distant sadness in his eyes, as though something inside him broke that day. "It's our only option. We don't have the resources to rebuild, and we don't have the numbers required to survive on our own. We'll have to take over the humans to stay on this planet."

Stathos-1 hid his smile. "It's for the best brother, we'll protect the planet."

As if noticing the direction they were headed, Stathos-6 snapped his head up in grit determination. "Only one colony, that's it. Then we continue to find a peaceful way to move forward with our lives, and our people, on Earth, is that understood?"

"Understood, *brother*." Stathos-1 grinned.

Today

William unclasped his hand and stretched his aged fingers against the kitchen table. Day's end was coming, and the desert sky displayed a most glorious show of colors through the small kitchen window as the sun set. Somewhere below the floorboards a heater kicked to life, whirring, groaning, and clicking to warm the house beneath their feet.

"The centuries that followed were a constant fight for survival." His words came out rough with emotion. "The Battle of Towton, Napoleon, Hitler... even the Salem witch trials. My kind had a hand in all of it." He hid his eyes behind his hands, and a single tear fell down his withered face. He sniffled and rubbed his arm across his face before taking a deep breath. "One by one, we gave up the fight. We defected from our kind. Most of us found love. We'd find a human body and live out our days in one person."

He paused. "I found my Miriam. She knew of course, what I was. She insisted I find a body that had nothing left to live for. So that I wasn't taking a life away from someone else. That's how I found out that our species can inhabit humans stuck in comas. People who would have never woken up otherwise. Miriam was comfortable with me taking this body. It would have died otherwise. Miriam was heartbroken that she couldn't have children. But she always wondered if our children wouldn't have come out entirely *human* anyway,... it's been five years without her-"

A cloud of darkness filtered over his face before he shook his head and changed the course of his words. "Our species had become the toxin, alongside the humans, and we resigned ourselves to live out our lives and die of old human age. We didn't deserve this planet. No one does. Earth... is better than all of us."

A small smile crept along his lips. "But I never thought I'd get the chance to see another one of my cousins before I died. I thought for sure you were from the mothership at first. Of course, they still think they can turn the tides of war, take over the planet. They hunt us down, try to get us to come back for the cause. But here you are, *obviously* in love with a human." He said with a wink.

Estrellas' cheeks warmed, and they glanced sideways at Talia.

Talia smiled at them before she looked away and spoke to William. "What do you mean earlier, when you said you could unscramble Estrellas, but they would then be able to find us?"

"Well, it's quite simple. You see, our kind can still communicate telepathically. We still sense each other as if we were one giant organism. But those of us who defected found a way to mask our signals with love, two becoming one. Turns out, love is the most powerful experience in the entirety of the universe." He looked to Estrellas. "You are all scrambled because your heart is torn. The more you jump in and out of bodies, the more you try to hold onto love. But without a clear direction, you become lost. You must find out what your heart is craving most."

He lowered his voice as if only wanting Estrellas to hear. "I'm close enough physically that I can sift through your thoughts if you wish. Clear up your memories to find out where your love first started to become divided. But if I do that, and your mind clears, and if your love isn't strong enough, you'll be linked right back to the mothership." His gaze turned dark. "And Talia." He nodded in her direction. "Will be seen as a threat to you."

Chapter Seventeen

Unwanted

Estrellas shivered with fear. What if William cleared their thoughts and put Talia's life in danger? They wouldn't be able to live with themselves. What other human could have divided their heart? The way they felt about Talia was so overwhelming they couldn't imagine ever feeling this way about another. But without answers, they would be stuck in Angela's body, and Talia would never forgive them.

Perhaps it was worth the risk. They could find a place to hide Talia first, then if they did end up back on the mothership, at the very least, they could find a way to give Angela back. Talia's happiness and safety was all that mattered to them anyway.

With their mind made up they said. "Okay, William, let's do it, start digging into the deepest recesses of my mind." Estrellas said, face set with determination.

"Wait!" Talia's voice went up an octave. "Just like that? We're going to risk a direct line to the mothership? Are we really ready for that?"

Estrellas warmed at the possibility of Talia being concerned for them. The worn kitchen chair screeched against the linoleum as they turned from Bill to face her. "We'll hide you first, I promise, no harm will come to you. At the very least, we can get Angela back into her body. I'll do whatever I can to make sure that happens."

When Talia's bottom lip quivered, it took all of Estrellas's willpower not to still it with their thumb. To not lean over and wrap their arms around her.

Talia swallowed thickly. "But...what if I never see *you* again?"

Estrellas's mind raced. They had only ever *hoped* that Talia was emotionally invested in them. But they had resigned themselves to believing that any care she showed them was caused by a combination of being concerned for her own safety and her desire to be reunited with her best friend. But now, for the first time, it dawned on Estrellas that Talia truly did care for them, possibly even as much as they cared for her. More than just an obligation to do the right thing by helping Angela's body. But perhaps those short moments they had together as Brad, and then their journey so far as Angela, had made some small impact beyond moral duty. The idea that Talia would miss them, possibly even *long* for them, did something to them that they could not put into words.

They reached their hands across the table and gently laid them on top of hers, and when Talia intertwined their fingers and squeezed back, Estrellas thought their heart might burst out of their chest.

"I do miss my friend." Talia spoke softly, slowly. "But if this is goodbye, then why rush? *Please* give me one week." She laughed and wiped a tear from her eye. "I know Angela would understand if she knew what I was feeling right now."

Hot damn!

Her words came out nearly a whisper, as if she was breaking an unwritten law by saying so. As if by giving Estrellas permission to stay in Angela's body, even if for a short while, she was betraying her best friend. "Just one week... to say goodbye. *Then* we make contact."

Estrellas was tongue tied. A hot windstorm full of butterflies swirled around inside them. *She wants more time with me.* Salty tears lingered on their lips and flowed down their chin. *How will I ever say goodbye to you?*

They smiled and nodded at Talia. "One week."

Bill stood more swiftly than they thought possible for a person his age and clapped them on the back. "Great!" His old deep voice boomed. "I could use the company!"

Estrellas looked up at him. "Are you sure, Bill? We could be putting you at risk as well."

Bill shook his head. "Nah, don't worry. Your head is so full of tangled spaghetti all mixed up with love sauce, there's no way the mothership is going to get a line on you." He smiled and whispered as if they were conspiring together.

"Besides, I do love me a good budding romance, gives me all the tingles." He wiggled his shoulders like a showgirl, winked, and shuffled off toward the living room. He gestured for them to follow him. "Come on ya lovebirds." He looked over his shoulder. "Let me give y'all the grand tour."

Estrellas glanced sideways at Talia and a little thrill ran through them when they saw a blush on Talia's features, her eyelashes fluttered just slightly against her cheeks when she looked down and smiled. The energy cycling between them was like a magnetic pull that Estrellas had a hard time fighting. They wanted to give in to the force attracting them together. To live in that small space they created that belonged to only the two of them.

Bill stopped at the stairs that led up, he gripped the handrail tightly and the old mahogany wood creaked with each careful step as he climbed. At the top of the landing, he opened a closet revealing extra blankets and towels. "Help yerselves to whatever you need in here." He closed the closet and moved down the short hallway, pointing to two doors on either side. "Those are the spare rooms, up to you's if ya want to use one er both." He turned again to look at them and waggled his thick white eyebrows.

Estrellas smiled but held back a laugh when they saw Talia look away.

Bill stopped at the first door and turned the knob, but the door stuck. He leaned his shoulder into it and using his weight the door cracked open. "Now this room don't connect to the heater very well, so it gets mighty chilly at night." He mosied over to the only window adorned with white dotted swiss, a sheer cotton fabric that had yellowed with age. "This window is busted. Y'all try to open it and it's gonna fall right outta the rails, so best to leave it shut."

They made their way back out to the hallway which made a sharp right turn, and Bill led them to the final door on one side and a blank wall in front of them with a long rope hanging from the ceiling. "That there's the restroom, takes a while for the water to heat up. And this rope here pulls the stairs down that lead up to the attic. No need to be going up there though, the floorboards are rotting." He took a deep breath and looked at them. "That's all of it! Make yerselves at home." He inched between them and headed back down the way they had come, hollering over his shoulder. "Bout an hour or so and I'll start us some supper."

The quiet that fell between them after Bill left was palpable. Estrellas could have sworn the air between them rose a few degrees. They cleared their throat. "I'll take the cold room. That closet looked stuffed full of blankets, I'll just bundle up."

Talia clenched and unclenched her hands at her sides, as if there were something she wanted to say, but fought the words from coming out. After a long pause she nodded her head and said. "Thanks. I appreciate that." She threw Estrellas a smile that seemed forced before walking away and going into her room.

The sound of a small lock clicking into place was like ten steps back, a freshly sharpened dagger to their chest. They were so thoroughly confused by Talia's mixed signals that their memory loss was becoming only one of many of their mental health struggles. They wanted so badly to tumble off the cliff, through the waterfall, and into the deep pool that was Talia's heart. They thought about knocking on her door and saying the first true thing that would come to their mind, whatever that may be. But they refrained, and instead pulled a couple thick blankets from the hall closet and brought them into their room, purposefully leaving the door open.

After making the bed, they sat and watched the bright moon and stars through the window. They were so tempted to open the window, to feel the night air against their skin, but remembered William's warning. The last thing they needed to do was break ol' Bill's window, especially after the hospitality he'd shown them. They decided the next best thing would be to go on a walk. They searched the bedroom closet and found an old mildly moth eaten, light pink sweater and pulled it over their head.

In the hallway, they nearly ran right into Talia.

"Oh." She exclaimed while catching her balance.

Estrellas reached for her elbow to help steady her. "Sorry, you okay?"

Talia let out a nervous laugh. "Yeah, just took me by surprise.

Estrellas quickly dropped their hand and cleared their throat. "Um, I was thinking of taking a walk, would you like to join me?"

"Ah-" She hesitated. "I was going to see if Bill needed any help in the kitchen."

Suddenly William shouted from downstairs. "I'm good down here darlin!"

His clear interruption elicited an unexpected bout of laughter from the pair of them.

"Yeah!" The old man shouted. "I can hear a mouse fart from down here, house is as old as I am, well, as old as this body is anyway-"

His voice faded and mumbled away from their ears as Estrellas clasped their hands behind their back and tilted their head. "Well, what do you say? Take a walk with me?"

Talia grinned. "Sure."

The night was clear, and the sky sparkled. The chill air stilled as they walked in silence. Nothing but the occasional tumbleweed or cactus dotted the long dead farmland. Behind the house stood an old barn with its large doors hanging open on weak hinges. Run down and rusted pieces of old farm equipment filled the interior.

Estrellas glanced to their side and saw the faintest cloud of breath spill from Talia's lips. The idea of herbeing even the tiniest bit uncomfortable in any form made their skin itch.

"Would you like my sweater?" They asked with concern laced in their voice.

Talia laughed, bringing forth more fog from her lips. "I appreciate the offer, but I'm the one who is actually wearing a jacket, all you have is that worn out sweater." For the first time since they started their walk, Talia looked at them when she asked. "Where'd you find that thing anyway."

Estrellas had to force air into their lungs when they saw the light from the stars above reflect in Talia's dark amber eyes, she glowed with warmth despite the cold that surrounded them.

They gave their head a shake. "Um, it was hanging in the closet in my room."

Talia stopped and turned her body to face them. "Estrellas!" She nervously chuckled, "You can't just take Bill's things without asking. I'm sure that was Miriam's and he's probably sentimentally attached to it." Her lips hung slightly open, begging to be warmed by theirs. "Next time, just... ask first, okay?" She said.

Estrellas nodded. "You're right. I should have asked first." But the only thing their mind could focus on was her. The way the tip of her nose had a pink tinge of color against the soft tan of her skin. The way her face was always framed in small curls no matter how hard she tried to tie her hair up into a smooth bun. And most of all, the way they could feel the racing of her beating heart when they stood close enough to her and when they placed their hand against her chest.

Talia didn't pull away. "Estrellas, please-" She closed her eyes as she spoke. "I'm already beating myself up, I don't need you to make me feel more guilty."

Estrellas whispered. "What do you mean?"

"I mean... " She hesitated, kicking dirt with the toe of her shoe as she talked. "I had this moment earlier... when I realized we were safe, even if temporarily, and had bought ourselves more time together. I was... happy. And that moment made me feel guilty. Because I should only be thinking about saving my friend. Saving her should be the one and *only* task on my to-do list."

Estrellas knew that they should pull their hand away from Talia's heart, but they took one last step forward, closing the inches between their bodies, only their faces stayed apart.

The softness of Talia's voice as she spoke melted them. "I make it a habit of not getting close to people, they only ever disappoint me. But that doesn't mean I don't feel things. And what I feel for you... I've only felt it three times in my life. It's strong-" She hesitated, "and I'm greedy for more."

Estrellas matched her whisper when they said. "What-who, do you feel these things for?"

She looked up from her shoes and directly into their eyes. "Isn't it obvious?"

"In case you haven't noticed, *obvious*, doesn't come naturally for me." A quiet laugh escaped them.

"It's you."

Talia's hot sweet breath warmed their mouth, so close for the taking, centimeters apart, their heart skipped a beat.

"I felt it for the first time, years ago-and again, instantly, the moment I met you, when *you* were Brad. I didn't notice it right away this time. I think my platonic love for Angela, and then my fear for realizing what you are, clouded the feeling. But it's clearer now than ever before. I can't explain it, I hardly know you-heck *you* hardly know you, but I am unequivocally and passionately in love with you."

Their knees turned to jelly and the world swooped around them. But Talia was their anchor. They latched their eyes on hers and held on tight. *Love.* They knew they were in love with Talia, but to hear her say it, to have their feelings reciprocated, was beyond anything they could ever dream of. Words failed them. They wanted to fill the small space that separated their mouth from hers, but just as they tried to place their lips on Talia's, she pulled away. The magnetic pull that drew them to her, was now reversed and pushing them away.

"I want to." She said. "But I can't cross that line again. No matter how badly I want to kiss you, that body you are inside of has not given consent. I won't. Please understand."

"I do. I understand." It was as if a bucket of ice poured over them, extinguishing the heat between them.

Worry creased lines in Talia's brow.

Estrellas smoothed the lines with their thumb and placed a gentle kiss on her forehead. "I love you too."

Talia fell into their embrace, snuggling her head against their chin.

Estrellas whispered. "I have to tell you something."

"Hmm?"

Their pulse kicked up like a racehorse on a track and they could feel cold sweat along their hairline. Too late to turn back now.

"You know how you mentioned you had this feeling only three times in your life and two of them were with me?"

"Yeah?" Talia asked quizzically.

"Well... I was also the third."

Talia laughed. "What do you mean?"

"You know at the white sands, when I had that vision?"

Talia nodded. "Um hm."

"It wasn't a vision, it was a memory. I was holding your hand, you were younger, maybe late teens, and I was a tall skinny white boy with a mess of dark hair."

Talia gasped and pulled away covering her mouth with her hands. She turned away. "Oh my God. Holy shit. Oh my God-Oh my God-Oh my God. Shit."

"Talia? Are you okay?" Worry tugged at their core.

She spun back to face them, her voice steadily rising. "Why didn't you tell me?"

Their words came out in a rush. "I wanted to. Right away, I did." They took a deep breath. "But I was scared it would damage you in some way. Take something away from the person who you have become. If you knew your first love wasn't who you thought they were-"

Talia began to pace, hands on hips, walking bath and forth as if her footsteps could reveal some hidden truth to solve all her problems.

"I loved that boy!" She suddenly shouted. "I gave him *everything*. And one morning, the day before *senior prom* mind you, he suddenly didn't know who I was. I didn't believe him of course! I thought it was his way of breaking up with me, you know, a new form of ghosting, pretending to not remember someone. I was *heartbroken*. I cried for *days*. My mother wanted to have an intervention, to put me in a psych ward!" She pointed a finger at them, fury in her voice. "YOU *broke me!*"

Tears were streaming down their face. Seeing her pain bubble over so furiously, so suddenly, was torture. "I'm sorry. I'm so sorry, Tal."

She started pacing again as Estrellas pleaded. "Please, I don't know what happened. I only know that if I could have stayed with you, I would have. Without a doubt. Nothing would have kept me from you if I could have helped it."

Talia spun to face them again. "You don't know that! You don't know anything!"

"Tal, please. I hate seeing you in pain. *Please*, tell me how to fix this. I'll do anything."

She bit her lip and shook her head. Placing her hands back on her hips she looked to the sky and sighed deeply. "I don't know. I don't know." She stomped past them and headed back to William's house.

Estrellas held back the sobs that threatened to overtake them, head hung low, and followed her back to the house.

Chapter Eighteen

Save Yourself

The night chill of the desert, so opposite from the scorching heat of the day, would not release their bones. Estrellas was certain she would be frozen like a mammoth in the ice age for all eternity until the day Talia's warmth would once again release them from their torment. Only her love, her attention, would be the archeologist that could dig through their mind, heart, and soul, to set them free.

She had ignored them all through supper. Avoided eye contact, only half grins and one word answers directed at Bill. They were sure that this isolation, this emotional torment would be their undoing. Like sand slipping through their grasp, so too was Talia falling away from them. They could see the distance in her eyes deepen. Feel the invisible tether that connected them, fade.

If only they could remember, then maybe they could explain. Maybe they could understand for themselves what was keeping them so emotionally torn, and therefore lost from their own memories. What other force could possibly keep them separated from *her*. She was everything, everywhere, all at once. She was the cacti searching the earth for moisture, finding the good when there was none. She was the feathers on a bird riding the wind in the sky, determined and unafraid. She was love, hope, faith, everything that they could have ever hoped to find in the entirety of the universe. To lose her, would be to lose life itself. Meaning. Purpose.

They sat in the kitchen long after dinner was done, alone. Talia insisted on helping Bill clean up. They pretended the kindness in her voice was directed at them instead of Bill as she scrubbed the dishes. They watched the warm soapy bubbles cover the softness of her skin, wishing they were the bubbles. Catching sight of the tilt of her lips as she smiled, sad that they were not the cause of her joy. Bill left the kitchen first to go to bed. When Talia hung the dish rag, then silently turned the light off and went upstairs, leaving Estrellas alone in the dark, they could not bring themselves to move. The darkness was like stone encasing their body in despair.

When their legs were stiff and their nose cold, they finally found the strength to move their body. Standing, slowly at first, then one foot at a time, climbed the stairs to their room. They glanced briefly at Talia's closed door before entering their room and shutting their door behind them. Estrellas took one shoe off at a time and buried themselves into the many layers of blanket, hoping the bed would swallow them whole and release them from their pain.

Sleep came heavy and swift.

"Sooooo... what do u think? Limo or no limo?" Talia asked.

He was so wrapped in his thoughts he hadn't even heard her.

"I'm sorry, what are we talking about again?"

Talia playfully slapped his arm and chuckled. "Prom, Sebastian! Are we doing this fancy or laid back? You know it's only three weeks away, we need to start making reservations. Are you renting your suit or buying? What colors do you think we should wear?"

He laughed, stopped, and grabbed her shoulders gently to face him and said. "Talia. Take a breath."

She closed her eyes and breathed in deeply through her mouth and released the air slowly through her nose.

"You're right." She said. "I'm just so excited! It's like everything is leading up to this!"

He chuckled again and wrapped an arm around her shoulder as they continued to walk to class.

"I'm excited too." He said before kissing her forehead lovingly. "Okay, so yes to a limo, my treat. I'll make reservations for 2 at Petite La Chateaux. I'll be buying my suit and I'll wait until after you've picked your dress so that I can match whatever color you fall in love with. You're going shopping this weekend, right? Does that all sound good?"

She sighed and smiled wide. "Sounds perfect. What would I do without you?"

He happily shook his head. "Well, I'm pretty sure you'd be running multiple nations and solving world peace if I wasn't distracting you with my baby blues." He winked a bright blue eye eliciting more laughter from Talia.

"Yo, Bass! Heads up!" Chad shouted from across the hall as he threw a football at Sebastian who pulled his arm from Talia's shoulders swiftly and caught the ball easily.

"You ready for tonight, brother?" Chad asked, panting as he raced to catch up to them.

Sebastian mock tackled him as he shoved the football back and rubbed his knuckles into Chad's hair. "More ready than you are!"

Chad pushed him away as he laughed. He pointed a finger at Sebastian as he backed away down the hall. "Tigers fight!"

Sebastian pointed back. "Tigers fight!"

Talia crossed her arms as they moved forward side by side. "Ugh, can you smell that?" Talia asked.

"What?" Sebastian replied.

"The male testosterone in this place, it's overwhelming." She smiled wryly at him.

He sidestepped in front of her, stopping her in her tracks. He pressed his lower body against hers and wrapped his arms around her lower waist, holding her tight and feeling the heat and softness of her body. "You know you like it." He whispered in her ear.

The soft intake of her breath and the warmth in her cheeks sent a thrill up his spine. He lowered his face closer to hers, rosy lips so close for the taking, cherry chapstick shining on the plumpness, the taste of her as familiar as if her lips were his own.

"No PDA in the halls Mr. Thompson." Mrs. Shepard said firmly as she passed them by.

Sebastian cleared his throat and pulled away. "Meet me after the game tonight?"

"Where else would I be?" She smiled at him.

He intertwined his fingers through hers as they continued their walk to class through the bright and sterile halls until the first warning bell rang. "Oh I don't know, curing cancer, becoming the next Van Gogh." He leaned a shoulder against hers. "You're capable of anything." He said sweetly, intently.

The bright stadium lights blinded him against the darkness that surrounded the football field. Cheers and shouts from the crowd rose to a steady hum. His hot breath steamed out in front of him like an affront to the cold winter night. Frost tipped the grass and his cleats were slick with melted ice. Nothing got his adrenaline pumping like the energy from game night.

As always, he sought her out in the crowds. Searched for her dark curls and bright honey eyes. He found her, watching him while she smiled and clapped, she became his anchor in the chaos.

The hit came hard and without warning. He could see the tip of his fingers and toes flying out in front of him as he flew up and fell hard back to the frozen ground. Sebastian cried out in agony. Something, multiple somethings were broken. His teammates surrounded him in a panic and somewhere in the distance a fight had formed between the two teams. Sebastian screamed out again in pain. Panicking from the sudden and overwhelming onslaught.

Teammates pulled off his helmet as he yelled out. Nothing could calm him until he saw her. Talia's face brought him relief. Her tears gave him the resolve to quiet his screams. When talk of taking a trip to the hospital started to rise up, he forced himself to hide his injuries.

"No. NO. I don't need a hospital, I'm fine. I just need to walk it off." Sebastian mumbled as he let Talia help him off the field.

"Bass, I really think we should go see a doctor." Talia said, concern and fear lacing her words.

"I'm okay, Babe, really, I promise. Can you just take me home please?" Sebastian fought to keep his voice from wavering.

It was hard to keep his eyes open on the drive to his house. He couldn't let his human parents know he was hurt or they would insist on a trip to the emergency room, luckily, his mom worked nights and his dad was out of town for the week.

Talia stopped in front of his house and put her car in park. "Bass, I'm really worried, please let me come inside with you?" Talia pleaded.

"Babe, I promise, I'm good. I just need to sleep. Please don't worry." He forced a smile in her direction. "I'll call you first thing in the morning, we'll have breakfast at Sunrise Sunset. Saturday's special is your favorite, right?"

"Right. But Bass-"

"Please, Tal. It's embarrassing for me, k, I'm alright. Let me just sleep it off."

Talia clenched her jaw. "Fine, but you can't blame me for worrying. You're home alone and what if you have a concussion? You should let me stay with you. I don't understand-"

Sebastian cut her words off with a kiss. Their internal flame instantly grew and Talia breathed deeply as she parted her lips to taste more of him. He was tempted to explore further, to give in to her, to ignore his injuries, gather her up in his arms and run her straight inside to his bed. It took enormous restraint to pull away from her. "See. I'm okay. I'll see you in the morning. Pick me up?"

"Okay." Talia said reluctantly. She leaned back toward him and gave him one last gentle kiss. "Love you."

"Love you too." He said as he stepped out of the car and gave her one of his charming winks.

Sebastian held himself together long enough to smile and wave as she drove away. The second she rounded the corner at the end of the street he collapsed. He could barely manage to whisper the words, "Beam me up scotty." before he lost consciousness.

His eyes were crusty as he slowly parted them. Home. He was on the mothership. The gray membrane walls that flashed with the muted color of the other Stathos's connected consciousness, were unmistakable. Stathos-6 hovered over him like a worried mother hen. Sebastian's tongue was heavy and his throat dry as he moaned groggily.

"Hold on." Stathos-6 said. "Let me grab you some replenishment fluids."

Stathos-6 turned away from him and filled a stemless crystal chalice with a neon blue liquid. He brought it to Sebastian's lips and he drank greedily. Stathos-6 wiped some of the dribbled fluid from his chin.

"We almost lost you. Your lungs had filled, you were drowning. Do you realize what would have happened if you

died in this body? I wouldn't have been able to retrieve your consciousness. You'd be gone. Forever." Stathos-6 shook *with emotion. "You must not be so reckless with your life,* Stathos-1."

"Come on, Brother. *We've faced many worse dangers than a simple high school football game.* Do *you not remember the* Middle-Ages? The *blood-soaked battlefields?"* A *dry* chuckle *escaped him. "I think we can handle modern day* sports."

"You're *risking too much in this assignment.* The *girl's father can be manipulated another way.* Let's *reassign you."*

"NO."

Stathos-6 *was taken aback.* "Your *mind is clouded.* You *will lose yourself to this human!"* He *spat.*

"I *will not!"* Stathos-1 *sat up sharply, steel in his gaze. "The girl's father is key to infiltrating the higher powers. I'm fine,* Stathos-6. *Know. Your.* Place." He *said, his voice full of disdain.*

Stathos-6 *had hurt in his eyes.* He *stood and harshly pulled away from the examination table, crossing his arms. "I have been following your lead for many millennia."* He *said with his voice sharp as ice. "It has been you who has led us away from our true nature.* You, *who have brought us close to darkness, and for what?* To *call this planet ours? Why?* When *we could continue to explore the stars, this planet will survive without our intervention and without our control."* He *crossed his arms and narrowed his gaze. "This has become greater than a simple determination to build ourselves a home on* Earth. Enslaving *the humans?* Just *as* Mother *had enslaved us?* What *will we lose of ourselves in the process?* Some *things are not worth fighting for."*

Stathos-1 growled, he shook with rage. "This planet is worth fighting for. She, is worth fighting for."

Stathos-6 flung his arms up in frustration, voice rising. "I don't recognize you anymore! I don't recognize myself anymore!"

"Then that is your problem, brother."

"I will not let you destroy our family!" Stathos-6 screamed at Sebastian, as he stepped into a transportation pod.

"What her father can do for me, for us, is invaluable. She, is my family now." Sebastian said coldly just before the eerie green light enveloped him, and then he was gone.

Estrellas woke with a start. Gasping for air and covered in a cold sweat. The scent of the old musty and dust covered furniture in the room filled their nostrils. They stared at the dresser across the room. Atop it sat an old black and white photograph of Bill and Miriam, smiling happily in each other's embrace. *That* is what was worth fighting for. Not power. They would give up a thousand planets if it meant keeping Talia safe.

Their spirit broke at the realization of how they first met the love of their life. Talia was only a mark. Only ever a mark.

The understanding that there was no other human that had divided the love in their heart. It was only their desire for power and control that fought against his love for Talia, scrambling their brain. But they knew now, there was no longer division. No longer torn between taking over Earth or loving her. It would always be her. They would always choose *her.*

If Stathos-6 knew, if only they could tell him, that they were finally on the same page. That they were no longer fighting for a takeover of the planet, maybe he would give up his chase. Is that why Stathos-6 attacked them back at the apartment? Did he think he was putting an end to an infection in the Stathos hive?

But pieces of the puzzle were still missing. Why did they leave Talia all those years ago? At what point did Talia turn from a mark into true love? And why were they reassigned into Brad, and then Angela's body? Was that at Estrellas's, demand? What was Stathos-6 hiding? Why did their memories still evade them?

Estrellas tossed and turned with questions unanswered until they fell back into a fitful and uneasy sleep.

Chapter Nineteen

End Of The Old Times

The previous night's dream had unlocked something in their subconscious, and like cracks in a dam, memories were slowly finding their way through the wall in their mind. Estrellas straddled a dangerous line. On one side they carefully and gratefully devoured every sip of love for Talia that their mind gifted them through old memories. But on the other side, they were tempted to take a sledgehammer to the blockade in their head and allow the flood of knowledge to drown them. And that temptation scared them. They were fully aware that if they let their resolve slip and they forced the unraveling, that Stathos-6 would have a direct line on their location; and they knew now that

Stathos-6 was capable of murder as a means to an end, whatever that *end* might be.

The midday sun was high in the sky, baking Bill's old wood house with stifling heat. Bill had his weekly appointment with a local charity that picked up the elderly from their homes to help them get their prescriptions filled, take them grocery shopping, and any other errands that needed doing. His absence left Talia and Estrellas walking on eggshells around each other. They opened all the windows and lounged in silence on the rickety and moth-eaten furniture in the living room, using old newspapers as fans and desperate for any slight breeze.

Estrellas would be miserable if it weren't for the expression they kept glimpsing on Talia's face. The anger from last night had faded, and in its place a mixture of what looked like longing and sadness. Their heart ached for her, and they hated seeing her in pain, but anything was better than the seething rage she had turned on them.

If only more recent memories would befall them. If only they had an explanation to give her, but so far, only small slices of the past had wormed their way in.

Talia's sweet voice broke the stale air.

"I'm miserable." She was laying across the loveseat in the corner and raised herself to a seated position. "It's been far too long since I've smothered my emotions with froyo." She stood with her hands on her hips. "I'm going to town."

The idea of Talia leaving them behind made their pulse fly. They watched her with anxious anticipation.

She marched across the room towards the front door and paused with her hand on the doorknob. She spoke over her shoulder. "Are you coming?" Talia did not wait for a response as she opened the door, leaving it ajar, and walked outside.

The shock of being invited froze them momentarily to the couch. After a beat they stood swiftly and hurried out of the house, closing the door behind them. As they climbed into the car, Estrellas could not fight the happiness that spread across their lips.

During the drive, they were grateful for the olive branch Talia had extended and scared of snapping it by saying the wrong thing, so they said nothing and watched the bright tan landscape flash by.

The smallness of the town made it easy to find a frozen yogurt shop. They pulled in. The place had a large parking lot full of small potholes and weeds growing through cracks in the asphalt. It doubled as a burger joint and despite the peeling paint and overall lack of apparent upkeep on the outside, the inside of the business appeared clean, well-kept, and lively through the large front windows.

A bell tinkled overhead when they opened the front doors, and the hearty aroma of fat rendered from beef and hot fry grease mingled with the lightness of spun sugar and fountain drinks, filling their nostrils. The sizzle from the grill combined with the hum of customers was so opposite from the quiet of the old farmhouse that their senses were on overload. Estrellas looked over to Talia who appeared to be waiting for an answer from them.

They stuttered. "Uh, oh, I'm sorry, what's the question?" They stared into Talia's eyes, so patient, so kind.

"I asked if you wanted to sit down and have lunch or take it to go." There was a slight clip to her voice.

"Um, whatever you'd like to do." They made an effort to drown out their surroundings, make eye contact with Talia, and grinned.

"Great, let's stay. The air conditioning in here is nice. Besides, it's too quiet at Bill's."

Estrellas nodded and smiled at her again. "Agreed." Their heart did a small tap dance at the slight rouge tint that blossomed on Talia's cheeks. *She can't help it, she loves me.*

"Dessert first?" Talia asked.

They chuckled. "Anything for you."

After ordering they found a small, secluded table for two and sat across from each other. Estrellas loved the way Talia took her time. The way she scooped small amounts of the creamy frozen vanilla into her mouth and slowly pulled the spoon out as if trying to taste every tiny morsel.

The ache in their chest lessened. Talia may not be talking as much as Estrellas hoped but she told sagas with her body language. She may not *want* to forgive Estrellas, but they sensed that she couldn't help it. The way she leaned close. The way she brushed their arm when she reached for a napkin, and the way her eyes spoke for her in a way her words could not.

When she had reached the bottom of her froyo bowl, she titled it up to her mouth to drink the last melted bit, and when she brought it back down, she had a satisfied smile on her lips and a patch of white on her nose.

Without thinking, Estrellas leaned across the table and cupped Talia's face with one hand while gently wiping the froyo from her nose with their thumb. Their soft brown hand lingered against Talia's warm skin until she pulled away.

"You can't do that."

Estrellas's hope sank to the bottom of their gut, as if the spell of their unspoken truce was broken. "I'm sorry, I wasn't thinking."

"Of course you weren't!" She looked around and lowered her voice, but the harshness remained. "You're never thinking about anyone but yourself."

"Tal-"

"Don't call me *that*." She glared.

"I'm sorry-"

"Just stop, *please*. I *try* to be the bigger person. I try to be patient, and understanding. But you just take and take, without stopping to think if you've had enough!"

"Tal, please, I don't understand-"

"Of course you don't, why would you?"

Panic coursed through their veins as they watched her shake her head while standing and gathering her wallet as if getting ready to leave.

"Wait. *Please*."

The desperation in their voice halted Talia. They stood and reached for her hands before stopping themselves.

"You're right. I'm selfish." They paused and gulped. "But I'm selfish for *you*. Selfish for your voice, for your smile, for any scrap of attention from you that I can get. I can only think about you, about what you're feeling, what you're thinking-" their voice dropped to a whisper and Estrellas took a step closer. "*If* you think about me, and *what* you might be thinking about me." They hugged themselves to keep from touching her. "*You*, are all I care about. And this divide between us... is *killing* me. I don't know what possibly could have happened to make me leave you all those years ago, but I understand now what I put you through, and 'sorry' will never be enough." They took a deep breath and let it out slowly. "Tal, my heart feels like it's broken in two and I can't breathe without you. *Please*, don't leave me."

The air between them vibrated and a single tear fell down Talia's cheek. Estrellas hesitated before slowly taking one last step towards her, and carefully wiping the tear away. When she didn't yell again or pull away, Estrellas pressed their forehead against hers and spoke softly. "I am forever yours. I will move mountains to be by your side. I will never leave you again without a fight to the death, because life is not worth having without you."

Fireworks exploded inside them when Talia dropped her head onto their shoulder. The air left their lungs when her arms pressed against their chest and she sobbed. Estrellas fully embraced her and held on tight, smoothing back her curls and placing a kiss on top of her crown. *I'm home.*

Chapter Twenty
Everything You Want

She hated herself-no, disappointment, she was disappointed in herself. Talia had always considered herself to be a good person, even from a young age. When that baby bird fell from a tree, she nursed it back to health; stayed up all night, set up heat lamps and gave it little droppers of food. And when that injured cat crawled its way to her front door after those nasty neighborhood boys thought they'd have a little fun with some fireworks, she rushed the cat to Mr. Jones, the town's veterinarian, convinced him to take her whole piggy bank savings for payment, and afterward turned those boys in to the local sheriff. Justice served.

Teenage years were even harder for Talia, her mom had pulled away emotionally for reasons she didn't understand and her dad was always working, but she held onto her desire to help others. She volunteered at the homeless shelter, the children's hospital, befriended every wallflower and so called, 'loser'.

Then came along Sebastian Thomas. Her world got turned upside down. She still considered herself a good person, but, Bass, made her selfish. Spending her time in his arms instead of volunteering. Befriending his friends and not spending as much time with her animals. And finally, going against her parents' wishes when they demanded she stop seeing Bass. She refused, and the fragile relationship she had with them, shattered.

Bass proved her parents right in the end. He abandoned her. Cut her heart with a knife clean in half. She became a shell of herself, moving through life in slow motion, barely registering the things happening around her.

Angela was the one who picked her up. She made her laugh again, and suddenly she was enjoying her art with a passion she hadn't felt in years. Creating magic and beauty with her hands. She didn't even care that her parents all but disowned her when she chose art history for a major, because she had Angela. They were each other's family.

Talia nearly lost her mind when one day a stranger was wearing her face. Had this alien been any other being, in their own skin, alien or not, Talia would have helped them with no questions asked and would have even roped Angela into whatever crazy situation they were in.

But here was this, ALIEN. Wearing her best friends' face. Why would any sane person befriend a body snatcher? And *it* was *obsessed* with her. She should have had some common sense, she should have run for the hills!

So why hadn't she?

It was this feeling. Somewhere deep inside of her, was a tiny warm butterfly beating its wings. The more time she spent with *them* the more her belly grew with warmth. Then her heart did something strange. It shifted. As if a tiny current of electricity ignited in her chest and began to flow through her veins, igniting spark after spark that could not be ignored.

But they were still wearing Angela's face. Touching Talia with Angela's skin. And her mind was still telling her that this whole situation was crazy, that at any moment *they* would reveal their truth and hurt her.

And then it happened. They did hurt her. But not in the physical way she expected, something much worse. They told her that *they* were not only Brad, the first person to make her feel hopeful for romance again, but also Bass, *her* Bass, and who knows how many other people? She nearly drowned in her own emotions.

She was scared-no, terrified. Talia was tortured with not knowing if she was doing the right thing by helping them, by trusting them. This was new territory for her, for anyone.

If it weren't for that tiny flutter that had grown, and the small spark that was electrifying every inch within her, she would never have helped this foreign thing.

Thing? No.

They were no longer a thing, they were *Estrellas. her*, Estrellas. No matter how hard her mind tried yelling at her, the love in her heart would dampen the screams. Soon, she wasn't seeing Angela as often. Soon, she was only seeing Estrellas, and that was scary. Talia refused to lose her friend, her *best* friend. She had to keep reminding herself that Angela still existed somewhere.

Suddenly, keeping Angela and Estrellas as two separate people in her mind was becoming more and more a battle of sheer willpower.

Finally, Talia realized that the only way to keep from losing her sanity, would be to give in. Let go of the fear and doubt in her mind, and trust her heart. Trust that warm baby butterfly that only continued to grow.

At that moment, she let her tears go and fell into Estrellas' embrace. It felt as though a thousand pounds had fallen from her shoulders.

She was home.

The sun was high in the sky when they left the cafe. Talia had a bounce in her step and a smile spread across her face. For the first time in days, she could breathe again. She could see Estrellas for what they really were. A good person that she loved. No matter how badly she tried to deny it, she was in love with Estrellas.

She knew she still could not cross that physical boundary. Not until Angela was back where she belonged, and Estrellas had their own body, but she also could no longer hide her feelings. This powerful thing inside her would not be shoved down. Talia embraced it. She savored it, licking every sweet racing pulse in her chest and sugared jellybean in her belly. It was as if something in their souls had called to each other. Estrellas was her person, human or not, and she was going to fight tooth and nail to help them win their freedom from the other Stathos's.

Her love for them didn't fully erase the ebbing fear that throbbed within her when her mind would quiet. Something was coming, she could feel in her bones. But with Estrellas at her side, she could face whatever was to come. They could take on anything as long as they had each other.

Talia buckled herself into her car and waited until Estrellas was secure as well. "So, what do you think about cooking Bill dinner for a change? Want to stop by the grocery store and get a few things?"

Estrellas smiled at her with an ease she hadn't seen before, peaceful maybe? "Yes. I think that sounds like a wonderful idea." They said.

Talia glanced in her rearview and side mirrors before easing the car out of the parking space, shifted to first and pulled out of the lot.

The warm desert air caressed her skin like a silken blanket blowing in the breeze. *I could get used to this heat.* Just as she was about to turn onto the street that led to the market, a sign caught her eye.

'Paintball wars, two miles' and a rainbow painted hand pointing to the right.

"Oh, we're definitely going!" Talia declared with excitement.

Estrellas narrowed their eyes in confusion. "I'm sorry, going where?"

Talia pointed to the sign ahead and asked. "Ever been paintballing?"

They laughed. "I can't say if I have. But if you're excited, I'm excited. Let's go!"

Five minutes later Talia slowed into a dirt parking lot. A banner made of colored triangles hung above a makeshift entrance held up by tall wooden poles. A one-person ticket booth sat behind it and a short girl with pixie brown hair, and bold glasses, wearing a dinosaur shirt, greeted them with enthusiasm.

"How can I help you?" She asked.

"Two please." Talia said.

"You are in luck, the next battle round is about to begin!" The girl said. "Are you renting any gear today?" She asked.

Talia laughed. "Yes, all of it."

"Coming right up! That'll be $45 each."

Talia handed over her parent's credit card. The girl rang them up and wrapped neon green nylon bracelets around each of their wrists. The girl disappeared from view and re-emerged from behind the ticket booth and wheeled herself over to a large table filled with equipment. She reached for what she needed and handed each of them a face mask, a sleeveless colored jacket with lots of stuffed pockets probably full of extra paintballs, and a paintball gun.

"Line up over there" she pointed, "and wait for the bell." She looked at Talia, "You'll be on the red team" then she looked to Estrellas, "and you'll be on the blue team." She maneuvered her wheelchair with ease when she rolled around them back towards the booth, then shouted over her shoulder. "Have fun!"

Hay bales were stacked into a maze formation seven feet high with two front entrances across a large open field. At least a dozen people grouped together near each of the entrances. Blue on one side and red on the other.

Excitement had Talia bouncing on her heels. She stuck her hand out towards Estrellas to shake. They took her hand, confusion etched on their face. "Good luck!" Talia said. She pulled her hand back and giggled as she hurried to her team. *They won't have any idea what hit them.* She thought as she laughed to herself. For just a moment, she thought maybe she should have explained what was happening to Estrellas. But they were a centuries old being, they could figure it out, and besides Talia rarely embraced a competitive nature, she needed this. She needed to blow off some steam.

Talia held the gun between her thighs, then pulled on her face mask and jacket. She tucked the gun under her arm and stretched her neck side to side. The bell rang. She took a deep breath and ran forward.

Past the entrance there were so many ways forward that her team quickly disappeared. She was alone. Talia's breath came in rapid bursts as she slowly peeked around each corner before running to the next place to hide. She stood and came face to face with a blue jacket, she shot, no hesitation, and ran on. Adrenaline coursed her veins pumping her body full of energy and drive to win.

She took out three more opponents before suddenly emerging from the maze into a more open obstacle course type space. It was chaos. There suddenly seemed to be far more people than she had realized. She rushed forward to a tall metal slab sticking out of the ground and took cover behind it. Paintballs flew in all directions. Splattering paint surrounded her. *I need to move.* Talia put the gun strap over her head and across her back then looked up. The tall slab had small holes perfect for climbing. She had to be fast, but had a chance, not many were looking up. She climbed. Moving her body as quick as she could, paintballs began exploding close to her hands but luckily missing her by millimeters. She reached the top and to her left was a stack of old tractor tires. She took a deep breath and jumped. The rubber surface of the tires made it hard to catch her footing, she slipped but managed to hang on, dangling feet above the ground. To her left was a wooden platform with two walls, perfect for a high vantage point with cover.

Talia swung her body side to side for momentum before flinging her body to the platform, her hands landed. She grabbed the wood boards tight, and pulled herself up to her elbows. She swung one leg up and onto the platform, pulled herself up onto her belly, and rolled behind the walls.

She lay there a moment, heart beating rapidly, she laughed. *I'm a badass.* She crawled on her stomach over to the edge and looked down. Identifying multiple targets, she pulled the gun from her back and began to aim. One. Two. Three. Four more hits before people started to realize where she was. Paintballs started flying up and she scooted back. She peeked again and saw someone climbing their way up to her. She pulled her gun forward again and aimed.

She was about to take the shot when she saw Estrellas further down below. One of her teammates had Estrellas in their sights. Talia shifted her gun to the left, aimed, and shot. She hit her target, her teammate and saved Estrellas, just as a paintball from the person who had climbed up hit her hard right in the facemask. Eliminated. *What the fuck was that?*

Talia couldn't explain why she saved Estrellas, her opponent, but some instinct seemed to take over and she had a sudden urge to protect them, sacrificing herself in the process. Somehow, she didn't regret it. In fact, she'd do it again. She lay there on her back breathing heavily and smiling.

After a few minutes she carefully made her way back to the ground, through the maze, and out to the front entrance. She returned her equipment and waited patiently for Estrellas to emerge.

Ten minutes later there they were. Strutting out with a crowd of blue's patting themselves on the back and pumping their fists in the air in victory. Happiness poured through her at seeing Estrellas so proud of themselves, so celebrated.

Estrellas looked around until they spotted Talia. They walked to her and stopped in front of her. "So, looks like I'm a natural." They said with a smirk.

"Looks like it!" Talia said happily. "Come on" she nudged them with her shoulder, "let's go get Bill some supper."

Talia woke with a start. Her room was dark, cold. She tried to slow her breathing. *What was that?* A noise had roused her from sleep. The energy in the room was... *off.*

Something's wrong.

It was as if someone was watching her, hidden in the shadows. She slowly placed her feet on the floor squinting into the quiet. Her heart beat in her ears.

Footsteps.

Heavy and fast.

Estrellas burst into the room. “He’s here. He found us!” They whispered urgently while pulling her to a stand. Eyes wild, they yanked on her arms dragging her out the room and into the hallway. They ushered her to the end of the hallway and pulled on the rope that brought down the attic stairs.

“Hide up there. I’ll lead him away. *Don’t come down until it’s safe.*” They said before urging her to climb up and shut the stairs hiding her from view.

Alone.

Cobwebs lined the rafters and floor beams, Talia, careful not to walk in between the beams on the floor, hurried to the far corner of the attic. She hunched down wrapping her arms around her knees and shivered in the darkness.

There was movement below her. She could hear Bill shouting and Estrellas grunting. Talia’s heart raced. Her jaw tensed. In moments debris on the attic floor rattled, a loud ear pounding sound filled her head. She pressed her hands against her ears and closed her eyes tightly. The whole house shifted and Talia was tossed into the wall. Pain shot up her back and her head made a sharp thwacking sound when it banged against the wall.

She screamed out.

Bright green light flooded up between the floorboards as if the whole house was exploding with light. Talia squinted against the sharpness of it. A thunderous clash exploded above her head and a giant gaping hole opened in the roof above, jagged around the edges, as splinters of wood rained down her.

Consciousness threatened to evade her as she was lifted by the light into the sky. Her teeth chattered and her muscles twitched until finally, she could no longer hold on.

Everything went black.

Chapter Twenty-One

The Mission

The cool night air pressed down on them like a weighted blanket as Estrellas lay in the dirt, blood trickling down the side of their mouth. They stared at the blackness of space until their eyes drifted to the pockmarked moon. So full. So bright. Clouds shifted across it like thin cotton caught in a breeze.

They moved their gaze to the side, looking straight into Bill's cold dead eyes, glossed over and somehow darker without the light of life shining through. He had fought valiantly up until the end, even in his human body, he fought, and lost-spectacularly.

Estrellas turned their gaze back to the moon. They had remembered everything. Not consciously, or willingly, no, the cracks in the dam shattered and it all came rushing back. It all happened so fast, they didn't even have time to warn her, to protect her.

Stathos-6 had been ready and waiting for the moment that he'd have a clear connection to them. He jumped. In seconds he was at their location and Estrellas knew in that moment that he had come for her, not them. He didn't have it in him to kill Estrellas, so he would do the next best thing-he'd use *her* to punish them.

The thought of giving into defeat crossed their mind more than once. It would be so easy to give into that feeling. To lay here until the wild devoured them like the lost soul that they were. Welcome the coyotes that howled in the distance, invite them to feast until their bellies were full. To stay in this exact spot and let their remains decompose until their bones were nothing more than a bump in the road covered over with a thick layer of dust and dirt.

But a vision of Talia's face floated across their eyes like a dream. The way her eyes sparkled when she smiled. Her hands like a phantom against their cheek, warm, and comforting, calling to Estrellas. They had to get up. She needed them, Estrellas was her only hope.

A deep groan spilled out their mouth like a waterfall, heavy and deep. Every joint cracked as they pulled themselves up to a seated position. Their left leg was twisted at an awkward angle. They gingerly reached forward. Estrellas grunted and a tear crawled down their face as their fingers prodded the damaged leg. They grabbed the leg tightly with both hands, clenched their teeth and twisted hard. Estrellas screamed out into the night a wail so deep it echoed off the hills.

They could feel microscopic organic alien tech filter to their broken leg. Like small intelligent lice with healing intellect and capabilities that burrowed into this altered human body like a friendly virus. They could sense as the tiny things went to work rapidly repairing the bone and tissue, stitching together their flesh piece by piece. As they sat there looking into the distance, the world appeared off, as if angled wrong. They realized their neck was hanging, lounging on their shoulder. They grabbed each side of their head and yanked it back into place. Heat flooded up their body as the microscopic organisms raced to heal the new area.

Estrellas took deep long breaths. They poked and prodded the rest of Angela's body seeking out any other major injuries in need of repair. A few broken fingers, an open bloody gash in their side, a missing toe and a few cracked teeth. They sat in that spot repairing the damage until they felt fixed enough to stand. They limped in the direction of the carnage that was once Bill's beautiful home, as their body continued to heal. Each step more sturdy, each breath more sure, their vision increasingly more clear.

Estrellas was back to full strength by the time they reached the front porch. The steps were split down the middle, huge chunks of wood were scattered about the area, and the entire house leaned to one side like the great leaning tower of Pisa. They carefully maneuvered their way around the wreckage and into the house.

Estrellas went room by room. Climbing over broken furniture, tossing tables and chairs out of their way. They reached the demolished stairs and stared for a moment before realizing they were impassable. Estrellas looked up to the second landing, crouched down, flexed their muscles, and lept straight up like a pouncing cheetah. They landed with a thud on the second floor, and the house groaned and shifted from the sudden weight. Estrellas held still and sighed with relief when the building did not crumble.

They carefully walked to what was left of Talia's room, tossing aside clothing and fallen dresser drawers until finally, they found what they were looking for. Talia's purse. Estrellas put the strap over their head and walked to the large gaping hole that used to be a window. They looked down for just a second as a breeze blew through their black hair, judging the distance, and jumped.

A small cloud of dust enveloped them as they landed unshaken. Estrellas got into the driver's seat, slid the key into the ignition and gunned it toward the direction of town. A mile down the road, a caravan of emergency vehicles passed by Estrellas. Their lights and sirens screaming as if they could scare away the danger in their path.

Estrellas settled into the seat for the long drive ahead of them. In twelve hours time, they would arrive at their destination, face the consequence of their actions, and beg for mercy.

Chapter Twenty-Two

Savin' Me

Several Years Ago

Sebastian and Talia held hands as they entered the high school. Smiling at their friends and nodding at acquaintances as they made their way to their lockers. Sebastian had bribed a freshman with promises to introduce him to Talia's best friend, Stephanie, in order to switch lockers so that he could be next to Talia-much to Stephanie's dismay.

Sebastian's resolve had been crumbling a little each day. The more time he spent with Talia, the more he doubted his intentions. He no longer focused on weaving himself into her family's fold for nefarious reasons, instead, he craved it for an entirely different reason, for their approval. They were no longer his pawns to be played with, they were the parents of the woman he loved, and he wanted their permission to do so freely and with their support.

Love?

Yes, he knew now, this was love. What a beautiful feeling. Warmth, desire, anxious butterflies encompassed all of him. He missed her when she wasn't nearby. The melody of her voice was his favorite sound, the color of her eyes-his favorite color. There was no other human, no other being in the entirety of the universe that held his heart in the palm of their hand the way she did.

He had lost sight of his obsession with world domination. Could no longer understand the point of it all when the Earth was plenty big to share. The angry fire within that had driven him for so long had finally been extinguished. He was at peace. Happy for the first time in his extraordinarily long existence.

Now he had a new mission... Talia. Building a future with her was all that mattered and ensuring a quality connection with her family was the key to doing just that.

Sebastian shoved his backpack inside his locker and grabbed the book he needed for the first period. He closed the door and leaned against it, head tilted and heart racing as he waited for Talia.

When she shut her locker and turned to look at him, she laughed.

He grinned ear to ear. "What? What's so funny?" He asked as he pushed off the wall of lockers.

Talia stifled her laughter and shook her head as they started to walk toward class. "You. Bass, you just had the goofiest look on your face, it was cute."

Seeing the blush on her cheeks sent the internal butterflies into a frenzy. The thought crossed his mind that he could power the whole school with the heat energy blasting through his body.

He smiled. "You, my love, are the *only* one who will ever get that look out of me."

Talia mocked bowed. "Well, it's an honor." She giggled as she tucked her book under one arm and grabbed his hand with the other.

He started to talk and hesitated. His hands were clammy and he felt tiny droplets of sweat beading on his forehead. Sebastian cleared his throat and tried again. "Hey, babe?"

"Hmm?"

"I think, I-umm." He cleared his throat again and spit his words out in a rush. "I'd like to meet your parents."

Talia squeezed his hand in shock and stopped in her tracks. "My parents? You want to meet my parents?"

"Yeah. I mean, don't you think I should?" He blushed. "I mean, do you want me to?" He ducked his head as if scared to meet her eyes, his hope so built up he was scared of that hope being dashed and crashing to the ground.

After seconds of silence he braved to look up. Talia was bouncing on her heels and smiling so wide he could see all of her teeth.

"I would love to introduce you!" She pressed her lips to his so fast he hardly had time to savor it. "How about

Saturday night? You can come over for dinner. Does that work?"

"Perfect." He said and nearly floated to the sky on a wave of pure joy.

The adrenaline and fear Sebastian had when he was preparing to face legionaries in ancient Rome on the battlefield, had nothing on the level of terror coursing through him now in preparation of meeting Talia's parents.

He carefully parked in Talia's driveway, smoothed the pants of his suit, and stepped out of his car.

Talia waited for him outside, next to the perfectly manicured lawn of the grand estate. A cool breeze lightly tossed her curls and she laughed when she saw him. "Bass. Why on Earth are you wearing a suit? It's just dinner with my parents, in our home, not dinner at a five-star restaurant."

Sebastian rotated his shoulders and cracked his neck in an attempt to ease his tension. "I just wanted to make a good impression."

She giggled again. "Oh, you'll definitely be making an impression, I'm just not sure of what kind yet." She winked at him and looped her arm through his. “Are those flowers for me?”

His heart sank.

I should have gotten two. Idiot.

“I’m sorry, love- they’re for your mom. Do you think she’ll like them?”

Talia nodded. “They’re beautiful, Bass-she’ll love them.” She leaned her head against him as they walked toward the front door.

They entered a large arched foyer with soft lighting. Two thick wood benches for seating and cubbies for shoes and jackets lined each side. In the corner there was a basket of bundled thick fluffy white socks.

Talia pointed. “We’re a shoes free home. You’re welcome to a pair of socks if you’d like.”

Talia sat down to remove her canvas shoes and Sebastian copied her. Talia grabbed his hand and led them down a marbled hallway that opened into an expansive sitting room. A wall of windows greeted them with a pristine view of La Jolla beach, a fireplace crackled in the corner warming the room, and light classical music sprinkled down on them from somewhere up above.

A man with silver speckled black curly hair sat with his back to them on one of the spacious leather sofas, legs crossed, arms rested, and ice clinking in his whiskey glass.

Sebastian had never seen Talia fidget before. She swallowed before speaking. “Ahem, daddy, our guest is here.”

A gruff sound of disapproval filtered to his ears. The man downed the rest of his drink in one gulp, and roughly set the crystal glass down. If a person could stand strongly, that would be how Sebastian would describe this moment.

Talia's father sucked all the power out of the room, as if the space were covered with a giant black cloth of electricity that was pulled up and towards the man as he stood. This person didn't *have* control, he *created* control with the energy of his presence. In all of Sebastian's years on this planet, he had only ever encountered this type of energy a handful of times. Stalin, Vlad, Hussein, Ivan the terrible, the only types of men who were ever of any consequence in the heat of battle. It was clear that this man was genetically programmed with the instinct to conquer, and conquer he would, he was already on his path to victory which was one of the reasons Sebastian had chosen him as a target to begin with.

In a snap, Sebastian was no longer craving the approval of his girlfriend's father, he was on high alert, staring at a high value asset that must be eliminated. His fingertips pulsed with energy begging to be expelled. Tunnel vision took over blurring out everything except the man walking towards him.

Talia's voice was distant, nothing more than a fly buzzing near his ears. "Daddy, may I introduce you to Sebastian Thompson."

Bass extended his hand, containing the baritone of his voice, jaw set, eyes narrowed, and forced smile exposing his teeth. "Mister Speaker, it's an honor to meet you sir."

The energy in the room sizzled and sparked. Talia's father grunted in reply for only a millisecond before his base nature sensed, much in the same way that wolves sense danger, that Sebastian was not just any boy trying to get into his daughter's pants. Undoubtedly his very practiced politician demeanor kicked into high gear. Mask falling over his face to hide any vulnerabilities.

I've got your number fucker.

"Sebastian!" The man's voice was full of deceitful welcoming warmth. "Good to finally meet you, Son. Talia doesn't talk of much else these days."

Sebastian felt the smoothness of his hand as he returned the shake.

No calluses, he has others do his dirty work, pathetic.

Sebastian relaxed the tension in his body and widened his smile. "Only good things I hope!" He forced a chuckle.

The tunnel vision receded as Sebastian eased into the situation he had stepped into. Talia was beaming on her tiptoes, apparently very pleased with how introductions were going.

The man patted Bass on the shoulder. "Come on Son, have a drink with me," he winked as if knowingly breaking the law by giving a minor alcohol would make them friends, "and feel free to call me Mr. Garcia, I'm at home, Son, not at work." He had a slight southern twang to his voice, not unlike the cartels of the past that Bass would toy with for fun.

This is going to be easier than I thought.

Sebastian laughed to himself as they made their way over to a drink cart in the corner.

"We'll take it easy on you, how about a little soda pop in your whiskey?" Mr. Garcia gripped Bass's shoulders giving him a little shake of solidarity.

"Sounds good, sir, thank you."

Mr. Garcia mixed their drinks as he spoke. "My wife should be down shortly," he paused, "she's been having headaches that leave her bedridden lately." He laughed. "You know, women, probably just the pain of having an empty nest soon, won't know what to do with herself." He winked.

Barf, this guy is toxic.

Sebastian smiled and took the offered drink, then followed Talia's father to the sitting area. Bass took a seat next to Talia on a loveseat across from the sofa Mr. Garcia sat on.

Mr. Garcia loosened the tie he was wearing and undid the top button of his collared shirt. "So, Sebastian, it's senior year, what are your plans for after graduation?"

Bass swallowed. "I have a full scholarship to Georgetown University, and I've secured a congressional internship, sir."

Mr. Garcia's eyes widened. "Impressive, young man." He looked at Talia. "My daughter failed to mention your accomplishments *off* the football field."

The way Talia's father looked at her was like a man angry at a secretary for failing to inform him of a morning meeting. As if she had left him vulnerable and let him down by not giving him all of the information. That look... made Sebastian's blood boil.

Asshole, I'm going to kill you slow.

A light airy sound tinkled from down the hallway. Talia's mother wore a chiming pendant, had long brown hair, was still in her pajamas and wearing a silk robe. She flitted down the hallway without a bother in the world. "Darlings-" she dragged the word out, "hope you haven't been waiting long." She said it in a way that made it clear she did not care how long they had been waiting. Her eyes were empty of liveliness, and her body language aloof, as if she were drugged, numbing herself to the limit.

Talia hurried over to her mother and whispered into her ears in a panic. "Mama, you promised you'd be on your best behavior."

Talia's mother brushed her off. "Oh honey, you worry too much." She wobbled over to the drink cart and poured herself a glass of wine as she spoke. "Besides, I'm sure this *boy* will be enraptured with you despite the state of your *mother*." She spat the last word and twirled to look at Sebastian for the first time. Her body stiffened; eyes wide with shock. "On second thought." She took a long swig of her wine and set the glass back down. "I think a good one on one interrogation may be in order-afterall, you are my *only* child." She looked pointedly at Bass, turned on a heel and walked back down the hall.

"Ah, Son," Mr. Garcia gestured to the bouquet in Bass's lap, "now may be a good time for those flowers." Sebastian nodded. He placed a kiss on Talia's forehead before he followed Mrs. Garcia, already out of sight, down the long hallway.

He found her sitting in a small alcove with two chairs, hands placed perfectly on her knees, waiting. Sebastian took a seat.

She leaned in close, eyes full of fire and spoke with controlled veracity. "I *know what you are, and you are not welcome in my home.*"

Sebastian leaned back, brow furrowed. "Excuse me?"

She pulled away with a maniacal laugh. "Oh don't fuck with me! I *know*. You will break up with my daughter, any excuse is fine, and you will never step foot near my family again."

"Ma'am-"

"Don't *ma'am* me-" A sharp intake of breath, her hand across her mouth, eyes wide. "Stathos-1? Is that you?"

Sebastian's mind raced. *How could she possibly know that*? He focused on his hive mind, searching for a connection to this woman sitting in front of him. There was nothing.

"How?" He asked.

Mrs. Garcia relaxed minutely. "Well, that answers that. You don't truly love my daughter, or you would know how."

He shook his head. "I don't understand."

She laughed, something sharp and shrill. "Of course you don't! You're pure *evil*. Always have been. Why do you think so many of our kind have been abandoning ship? Did you think *that many* are dying in their human forms? You really think we're so careless?"

Bass narrowed his eyes. "*Who* are you?"

She scoffed. "You'd forget your partner so easily?"

His pulse ticked up a notch, breathing short and fast. "Stathos-2?"

She held his gaze, a curt nod.

"I...I-thought you died."

"Of course you did. You single minded fool. If you stopped, for just a moment, and took notice of the beauty that humans could behold, then perhaps you'd see this planet for more than a simple thing to be conquered."

Bass shook his head in disbelief. "I still don't understand, why don't I have a mental connection to you?"

She sighed deeply, letting her air out slowly. "Because, Stathos-1, you will never know love, and because of that, you will never win." Something akin to sympathy flitted over her eyes, "Although, I can't deny the change in you, a shift *has* happened..." She seemed to be having an internal debate before she continued. "It's love, Stathos-1, true love. It's the key to everything. Our species has searched for autonomy, independence from the hive mind, for freedom; and love is the answer." She paused again. "If you really love my daughter, you'll let her go. Abandon this mission and never come back."

The cogs in his mind worked overtime, analyzing her words, turning them over and over until he finally understood.

"True love with a human, breaks the connection to the hive?"

She nodded, her lips were pressed so tight together they appeared as one straight line, as if she regretted the words that she had spoken, regretted sharing her secret.

He sat there processing this new information, and how it related to him and Talia. If he was still connected to the hive, did he really love Talia? He must. He'd never felt anything like this before. This feeling that she inspired in him. The curve of her lips, the smile in her eyes, the compassion in her heart. He loved her. Despite what Stathos-2 was telling him. A light bulb sparked in his memory.

He stiffened before he spoke. "You're hurting her."

Her eyebrows drew together. "What?" She shook her head. "What are you talking about?"

"Talia. She told me about how close she was to her mom, and how one day, her mother changed, was cold, and distant. Her heart breaks for the person her mother used to be. She misses her *real* mother. You *stole* this family. How can that possibly be love?"

She stood swiftly, anger laced her features. "That *simple girl*. Of course I don't love her, I *tolerate* her."

Anger thrummed through him. *How dare she*. Destroying the heart of the woman he loved. Tearing her mother away from her. Sebastian wasn't evil, *she* was evil.

She growled out her next words. "It's her *father* that I love."

Sebastian scoffed. "That toxic piece of man-shit!? That's who you fell in love with?" He shook his head in disbelief, laughing. "Oh Stathos-2 you always were a *fool*." He paced the small alcove. "I don't know what is breaking the connection to the hive mind, but it isn't true love. Look at you! You're obviously miserable. What are you taking? Hmm? Valium? I bet you're taking, what, six a day? You could barely walk until the sight of me sobered you up! You think that's fucking love?" His pacing increased, hands on his hips, he pointed at her. "You are the fucking problem, not me. You've abandoned your true family. You will die in that body, and for what? A noxious politician with a small dick!?" There was menace in his laughter. "Have fucking fun with *that.*"

Stathos-2 spat in his face. "How dare you." Fury laced her voice. "Get the fuck out of my house, *now.*"

He resisted the urge to snap her neck where she stood. She must have sensed the change in his body language, she cowered. He thought of Talia. His beautiful, innocent, loving soul of a human that he would do anything for, even if that meant letting this pathetic defector before him live. He tried to think of the Stathos-2 he remembered. The powerful one. So strong, she was capable of taking down entire empires. His reliable number two, his partner.

He calmly sat down and looked at her with softness in his eyes while he waited for her to sit as well.

When she finally did, he spoke. "I'm sorry, Stathos-2. I seem to have forgotten that we were allies."

She sighed with relief. "I didn't exactly welcome you with open arms." She rocked slightly in her seat. "And you were right. I fell in love with him before I realized who he was. Now I self-medicate just to avoid being near him." She hesitated. "I don't hate, Talia. I'm jealous of her, of *his* love for her and not me."

As if a sudden desperate realization came over her, she grabbed his hands and stared wildly into his eyes. "Does Stathos-6 know?"

"Know?" He tilted his head. "Know of what?"

She gripped him tighter. "Talia. Does he know of your love for Talia?"

"What does it matter?"

She dropped her head onto their joined hands before taking a deep breath and looking back up. "You oblivious imbecile-"

"What are you talking about?"

"Stathos-1... I followed you into battle for all those years, not for a thirst of blood or power, but because I knew, deep down, that you thought you were doing the right thing. You saw the corrupt nature of man. You saw the beauty of this planet, and you decided to take it, not for yourself, but for us, for your hive. I knew there was goodness in you, perhaps buried deeply, but it was there. If this girl has brought that out of you, then you must protect it at all costs."

She stared intently at him. "You *must not* return to Stathos-6."

He furrowed his brow. "Why? Stathos-6 has always been the best of us, the most levelheaded. He always tried to convince me that we could live in harmony with the humans. *I'm* the one who sent us on a warpath."

Stathos-2 released his hands, a soft laugh escaped her lips. "You beautiful idiot." She shook her head. "Stathos-6 is in love with you, obsessed even. If he can't have you, no one can, he will burn this world down when he discovers how far you have fallen for this girl."

Stathos-1 jumped up as if he were shocked by a taser. "No." He shook off an uncomfortable shiver. "No. He would never. He'll be thrilled that I've finally given up the fight for Earth. He will welcome her with open arms." He started to pace again, "You'll see. This is the turning point. This is our fresh start."

Stathos-2 stood, gently placing her hands on his shoulders to calm him, and whispered. “You’re wrong Stathos-1. And when you realize that, it will be too late.” She stepped back and ran a hand down her face. “I will help you. You were right about one thing. I was a fool to fall in love with this man. I’ve been by your side for a millennia, and I will stay by you until the end. We must end Stathos-6 if you want any chance at a future for yourself and for her.”

He backed away as if she had slapped him. “*End* Stathos-6? *Never.* I will not.”

She closed the space between them, leaning in close. “Mark my words, he will be the *end* of you and *her*.”

Several Years Ago, later that night.

Stathos-1 paced in his room. He had just gotten home from dinner at Talia's parent's house and thought about the warning that Stathos-2 had given him. She was wrong, he was sure of it. Stathos-6 was going to be thrilled that he was giving up the fight for Earth, to finally have peace. It didn't take long for him to make up his mind. He was going back to the mothership. He would tell Stathos-6 goodbye, that he was going to live his last life on Earth, with Talia.

Lucky for him, Sebastian's parents were rarely home. They never noticed that their son had frequent alien abductions.

He laughed to himself, shaking his head.

Alien abductions.

Stathos-1 opened his hive mind, he reached for the mothership, for Stathos-6. He found the mental thread and tugged on it. "*We need to talk, pull me up.*"

A green light enveloped him, and he slowly lifted and disappeared, only to reappear slowly on the mothership.

Stathos-1 was in his preferred type of body, young adult Caucasian males. He was currently in between missions, waiting to see how things played out with The Speaker. He greeted Stathos-1 with a smile. "How'd dinner go?"

"Great! I'll be part of the family business in no time." He hesitated and gulped. "About that though, there's been a change of plans."

Stathos-6 raised a brow. "Oh? How so?"

Stathos-1 looked toward the observation deck. Stathos-6 had a visual of the whirlpool galaxy pulled up on the wall of the ship. Exquisite sprays of purple stars spread out like sparks from a flame swirling together like magic stardust. Part of his heart missed exploring the universe, discovering new galaxies. But the stronger pull was his love for Talia. He finally found a home, with her, and he'd be damned if he was going to let her go.

He looked at Stathos-6 and saw him stiffen.

Shit.

Stathos-6 clenched his jaw. "If you're about to say what I think you're going to say-*don't*."

Stathos-1 held his hands out, pleading. "You've been right-all this time, I should have been the one following you, on your journey for peace and co-habitancy on this planet, for me, for us, for our kind." He paused, gulping for breath as the air was sucked from the room. "I'm not leaving you, we'll always be-"

Stathos-6 held a hand up and turned his face away. "The *things* I have done for you, for the *mission*- and one human girl is going to make you abandon it all, *abandon me*?" He began to pace. "I won't let you do it, I WON'T LET YOU LEAVE ME!"

His sudden shouting jolted Stathos-1 out of his euphoric hopeful bubble of love. The hairs on his arms raised, the feel of spider legs crawled up his neck and burrowed in his scalp. Then the anger bubbled up from his toes until his face was hot with self-justifying indignation.

"YOU FORGET YOUR PLACE!" Stathos-1 clenched his fists. "*You*-" he pointed, "would be nothing more than a thought, a spec, a miniscule cell on the origin ship without *me*!" He stalked the room back and forth. "I was the one who woke you. I was the one who gave you a life!"

Without warning Stathos-6 rushed forward and pushed Stathos-1 so hard he flew back, hitting his head against the wall with a hard smack. Stathos-6 shouted. "AND *now* you would take it away!? Just as easily as it was given, you would end my life?"

Stathos-1 felt behind his head and his fingers pulled away covered in thick crimson. He struggled to form the word with his tongue. "I am not taking your life. I'm simply giving you the chance to live one of your own, independent of me."

The tremors in his hands came slowly, thick emotion balled up in his throat. "I'm giving you your freedom."

"KEEP YOUR FREEDOM!"

In two swift steps he reached for Stathos-1's throat. He clamped on tight and lifted him off his feet as he spat the words. "You will be with me, *or no one*." He dragged Stathos-1 to the next room.

Stathos-1 knew he should fight back, his pulse raced and his teeth ground together in frustration at the weakness of this human body. Hot blood trickled behind his ears and down his back as his toes barely scraped against the floor while he was dragged.

Stathos-6 slammed him up and onto the cold metal slab that stood raised in the middle of the room. He strapped Stathos-1 down tightly and shoved an organic tube up his nose. Stathos-6 could feel the tube wiggle on its own accord, up, and up, until it spread its spindly vines out and around his brain, clamping on tight.

His back curved up in pain, leg muscles taught, as tears sprang to his eyes.

Stathos-6 stood over him, a cruel smile spread across his lips. "I've been *experimenting*, don't worry, you won't remember this."

Stathos-6 drifted in the background, Stathos-1 could vaguely see what looked like a large syringe full of pink goo.

Stathos-6's voice crawled with malice. "You and I will have a new mission." He stared him down, his cold eyes darkened black. The Stathos-6 he knew was gone, broken. He felt a prick in his neck followed by fire pouring through his veins. "We are going to find out *how* our family is leaving us, and we're going to get them *all* back, so that *no one* can ever leave us again."

The room blurred no matter how hard Stathos-1 fought for consciousness, Stathos-6's voice was fading, the last words he heard...

"We'll be together forever."

Then, darkness.

Chapter Twenty-Four

Jumper

Today

DENIAL.

That's the first stage right? Estrellas thought to himself as he drove across the country, only stopping once besides gas refills and restroom breaks to purchase some new clothes, and food. How could he have been so naive? No. Not naive. Overconfident, cocky, conceited, smug-just fucking stupid. All these years, millennia, Stathos-6 had been wrapped around his finger, like a puppy dog licking up his scraps. He'd been buried so deep in his ego that he had failed to see when Stathos-6 had begun to fight back. Now, it was too late. He had *her*. Stathos-6 was going to win.

I grew a conscience too late.

Fuck.

Night had fallen by the time Estrellas carefully pulled into Talia's parents' driveway. The fog had crawled in from the ocean and swirled underneath the glow of the streetlights like a strand of seaweed waiting to strangle him. If her parents didn't do it themselves, Estrellas was sure to choke on his anxiety.

He sat for a few moments in the silence of the dark strumming his fingers on the steering wheel, slowly forming a plan. He not only had his memories back, but Angela's, and with both, things were much clearer. The only thing he knew for certain... *fate*, wanted him and Talia together. Time and time again the universe thrust them together, and how he ended up in Angela's body was no exception...

Angela was hopeful for the first time in months. Dating apps, it turns out, were a cesspool of experimental college kids, cheating spouses, and people just looking for a free meal. Finally, she had found a good one. Jeremy wasn't exactly her

type, but what he lacked in melanin he made up for with excellent manors, charm, and ambition. He didn't want to live in his father's powerful shadow as a politician, he wanted to break out on his own, as a formidable healthcare attorney, determined to make the system better, just like her.

The date was going so well, not only did he actually walk to her door and knock to pick her up, and not just honk from outside or share the cost of an uber, but he also asked to pay for dinner at the best restaurant she had ever eaten at. He didn't insist like some testosterone fueled alpha male, or even worse, insist that she pay like some uneducated dumbass because she was a quote unquote feminist, he actually said he would like to pay and asked if that was okay with her. I mean talk about swoon worthy, that had never happened before, the closest were dates that offered to split the cost.

Neither of them wanted to end the night, so they decided to take a walk to the ice cream parlor down the street, which was perfect because she had promised Talia she would pick up a gallon of french vanilla with black cherries and caramel. And when he asked if he could hold her hand, she thought she might just float to the stars.

They were about a block away when they came across a blocked off section of the sidewalk where some construction was happening during the day, they would have to go around the back alley to get there.

Suddenly a bright green light illuminated the darkness around them from above. Angela tried to block the light as she looked up squinting. A loud groaning and whirling sound started coming from the light, like something huge and mechanical warming up. Her heart raced and she had trouble breathing. Jeremy slowly dropped her hand as he became entranced in the light and before she could understand what was happening, they were both being sucked upwards into the sky.

Brad was having a hard time focusing, his mind was all muddled. He knew he wasn't really Brad, he was something else. Spencer had said he needed an assessment, no not Spencer, Stathos-6. Something was wrong. He didn't know what it was, but he knew he needed to fight. He was on a slab, some tall gray humanoid figure was standing over him, but then it went out of view and came back, and the figure was now a bi-ped giant lizard, no not a lizard, Stathos-6 inhabiting a lizard.

Then he was rolling him to a different room where there were two bodies in a tube, a white male and black female.

Stathos-6 was saying something about the male being the son of some prominent politician. He rambled something about two humans being on a date, but the male wasn't alone often enough and he took the risk and abducted them both.

Brad realized then, he was supposed to be reassigned to this male. If that's what Stathos-6 wanted, then he couldn't let that happen. When the transition began, he focused all his energy, all his consciousness on going inside the female next to him, not the male as intended.

When Stathos-6 realized the switch he must have been infuriated. There is a short window of time when a soul can't be retransferred immediately, or there is a risk of shredding the consciousness, the soul. Stathos-6 would have been forced to return Jeremy's body, and must have kept Estrellas inside Angela until he could find a suitable replacement, not realizing who her roommate was.

No wonder he attacked them in the apartment. He must have lost his shit when he figured it out.

Fate.

Estrellas and Talia were meant to be.

With his memories freshly returned, he was able to piece together that the pink goo Stathos-6 had formulated acted as a type of mind wipe, but it wasn't permanent. Every time Estrellas was forced into one of his '*assessments*' he became *almost* a blank slate. He counted about twelve different assessments over the years, far too many. If only he was able to fight back sooner, he wouldn't have lost so much time with Talia, she wouldn't have had to go through so much heartbreak. It was of no consequence now, getting Talia back was the only thing that mattered.

He lay his head against the steering wheel and sighed deeply.

Time to face the music.

When he raised his head, Stathos-2 was in his eyeline, staring him down through the windshield like he was a petulant child in need of a good time out.

Arms crossed, she walked to his door and knocked on the window. "You coming inside, or you just going to sit there stewing in your misery?" Without waiting for an answer, she walked back up to the house and left the front door ajar.

The estate was warm and inviting, a clever mask for the real energy in the home which was a mix of self-loathing and excessive pompous pride. He shrugged off his coat and shoes and followed the long hallway to the sitting room. It looked the same, with the exception of some new decor. Stathos-2 sat on the sofa with her back to him staring at the night view of the beach, the waves crashing against the shore reflecting the moonlight, a wine glass in one hand, waiting patiently for him to join her.

He sat across from her. "Where's Mr. Garcia?"

"Gone." She set her glass on the table before her. "His nights are spent in the beds of varying young girls." She said it in a way that made it clear she had resigned herself to this reality quite some time ago.

They sat in silence and the minutes ticked by. Estrellas didn't know where to start, he was bouncing the balls of his feet and wringing his hands.

She picked her wine glass back up and took another swallow. "Why are you here Stathos-1, you know there's only so much I can sense, you will have to speak eventually. Nice new body by the way, I haven't seen you inside too many females."

He hung his head low as he laced his fingers behind his neck, his words came out stilted, trying to hold back the wave of despair that was trying to flood him. "He has her, Stathos-6 has Talia." He looked up, felt his tears hanging on the lids of his eyes. "I need your help to get her back, *please.*"

She leaned close to him and said with spite in her words. "And why would I do that? Hmm? Why would I risk *my* life when I warned you, told you to stay away from Stathos-6."

He enclosed his hands around hers that were gripping her wine like a lifeboat. "*Please*, I am begging you. I can't save her without your help."

She pulled her hands from his, spilling wine on the white carpet where it splattered like a blood stain. "What *is* it with you and this human!?" She set her glass down roughly and stood with her arms crossed, glowering down at him.

"I *love* her." He rose and placed his hands on her crossed arms, heart beating wildly against his ribs, pulse throbbing in his ears. "In all our years, Stathos-2, I have never felt what love is. I need her, to be able to breathe again, to live again. I am incomplete without her." He squeezed her. "Damn the planet to hell without her in it!"

Tears fell down her cheeks as she pulled back and wiped them away angrily. "It's not fair, Stathos-1! You think I don't crave what you have found! And if I help you, I'll never have a chance of my own to find it." She shook her head. "You know I won't come out of this alive."

"That's not true. I don't know that, and you don't know that."

"Oh, but I do. I do know it, Stathos-1, we won't all walk away from this."

If only he had the air in his lungs to scream right now, he'd rattle the walls. How could he ask her to lay down her life for him? But Talia was all that mattered. He had to save her.

He turned away, running his fingers through Angela's thick black hair, bowing his head, and desperate words falling out without remorse. "You're right, I don't know that we'll all come out of it alive. But I have to try. I won't force you to help me." He paused and turned back to face her, words cold and calculating. "But I would remind you, that your key to a new life is on that mothership." His brow raised and a smirk threatened to tug his lips, he held it back and said. “You could have a fresh start, a new body, a new path.”

Her bottom lip quivered, and she sucked it in between her teeth.

He spoke gently. “You don’t have to be trapped in this home. Help me. Get us on that ship and you can start again.”

Slowly, he walked towards her and placed his soft brown hands lightly on her crossed arms, covered in a buttery soft white sweater. “Please, Stathos-2, you’re the only other one with a connection to get us onboard without detection. I need the element of surprise, it’s the only way.”

She sniffled and wiped away her snot and tears on her sleeve, then nodded. “Okay, I’ll help you.”

Chapter Twenty-Five

The Kids Aren't Alright

He was back on board the mothership for the first time in weeks, and it all felt... foreign, not like a place he had ever called home. The soft tissue walls vibrated and smoothly pulsed faint light, like a silent alarm alerting the true inhabitants that there were intruders in their midst, it wouldn't take long for the hive mind to alert Stathos-6.

They were in an intersection, a clearing of sorts. The tunnels that crawled off in all different directions, up, down, and to the sides, were more dark than lit, wide in some places and narrow in others, like being inside the chambers of a bloody beating heart. Long fungus-like strands reached for him, little slimy hairs full of static electricity seeking out anything to attach themselves to.

Stathos-2 stood shivering and eyes wild next to him. "Ya know, on second thought, I don't need a new body, this one is just fine." She twisted her hands. "I got you here, now, I'm out."

Estrellas, holding The Speaker, Mr. Garcia, unconscious in Angela's arms, as easily as if he were nothing more than an infant and not a full-grown man, looked at Stathos-2 sharply. "You will not leave me now." His words rang with the finality of a cross mother putting their child in timeout.

They had too much history for her to abandon him. He had saved her life more times than either of them could count. Blocking a sword during the battle of Marathon. Pushing her out of the path of a war elephant during the battle of Zama. Everything from taking the brunt of the impact during a car collision, all the way to shooting in the head a vengeful and sneaky lover during one of her less than ideal assignments to a drug lord.

His face softened when he saw the pitiful trapped look coming from Stathos-2. With a kind voice he said. "It's been a while since we've had to fight, huh?"

She shrugged her shoulders, and Estrellas tried a new topic of conversation as a way of a distraction. "I mourned your death you know."

She had a regretful look on her face, as if saying 'sorry'.

He gave her a sad smile. "How did you end up falling in love with The Speaker? Seems like quite the serendipity seeing as how I was later assigned to his daughter."

She looked up with her hands on her hips. "To be honest, I'm not sure I ever really loved him, passion for a time, sure." She paused. "Do you recall? It was my idea first to infiltrate the Speaker's life, but I was overruled, told it was too big a target at the time. Of course, a while later, when no one was looking, I took matters into my own hands." She laughed and shook her head. "I abducted Talia's mom, hid her consciousness elsewhere on the ship for safekeeping," she waved her hand in the air like she was merely relaying a task list and not messing around in someone's life, "and planned on gathering some reconnaissance to bring back, to prove it was a good plan. But suddenly, and don't ask me why, I saw what this planet could offer besides just a place to live." She glanced at him sideways. "For the record, I knew Stathos-6 had his issues, but I had no idea what had happened to you, or I would have returned." She gulped. "Probably... maybe-certainly." She chuckled uneasily before continuing. "My severance to the hive mind must have been right before your assignment to Talia, I don't think the cause is love, I think-"

The light from the walls turned up a notch, and the long fungus-like strands doubled their efforts, waving around crazily as they extended their reach for them.

"Showtime." Estrellas said and adjusted his hold on Mr. Garcia. Stathos-2 switched into soldier mode, pushing the version of her that could be vulnerable in front of Estrellas, down and away. Face stoic and feet firmly planted, a warrior once again.

His voice, Stathos-6, rained down on them from all directions like surround sound speakers on full blast. "TRAITORS!" He bellowed, except his voice was all wrong, broken, raspy and wet. Silence. Heart pounding. Listening strained. Then crunchy slippery sounding footsteps that echoed to his ears as his figure slowly emerged from one of the many tunnels. Cloaked in a long-hooded robe like the penitent brothers they encountered once during Catholic holy days, except this cloak was dark red and lacked a masked face.

Fitting.

Stathos-6 stretched his arms out wide to the sides of the tunnel he was coming through, relishing in the touch of the fibroid-like strings calling out to him as though they carried him more than he walked. Their brothers and sisters, imprisoned and waiting to be released into a body. Emerging from a tunnel that slanted upwards, clinging onto the sides like a spider in its web, Stathos-6's figure became clearer as he got closer. He wasn't wearing a human body; he was in a lizard suit. It's skin, thick, rough and slimy, and height twice as tall as the average human. Red glowing vertical slits for pupils narrowed at him.

"You would return for that human?" Its ragged voice snarled at him. Stathos-6 turned its lizard head like an owl, no neck, towards Stathos-2. "And you. I thought you were dead." He looked back at Estrellas. "No matter-"

"Stathos-6." Estrellas said firmly, loudly. "I've come home to you, my memories have returned and I have seen the error of my ways." He took a step towards Stathos-6. "And I've brought a peace offering." He unceremoniously dropped Mr. Garcia and his body rolled to Stathos-6's feet. "I'm sorry Stathos-6, for allowing myself to be led astray, from the mission... from you."

Bile built along the back of his throat as Estrellas forced the words out.

"LIAR!" The lizard sprang towards him, knocking Estrellas to his back, its long, split tongue was hot as it shot into Estrellas' ear, paralyzing his human body in seconds with its toxins. Stathos-2 charged, and Stathos-6 effortlessly swatted her away, as if she were nothing more than a bothersome bug. She landed hard and unconscious.

Why'd he have to be in a lizard suit? We're fucked.

Estrellas' heart raced within his frozen body. Tension built with nowhere to go.

Stathos-6 grabbed a handful of hair the painfully pulled against his scalp, and dragged Estrellas across the ship. "You want your human so bad?" He rasped. "Allow me to bring you to her." Stathos-6 kicked The Speaker's body out of the way. Keeping one dactyly claw tight on Estrellas' hair, the other clutched a handful of fabric on his back; sharp talons pierced through his clothes to scratch against his soft human skin. It leapt up a diagonal tunnel and heaved Estrellas along like an oversized piece of luggage.

The long stretch twisted and curved like the real inner workings of a putrid beehive, hundreds of minds were the bees, buzzing within the walls, until they clambered out into a different kind of chamber, all smooth, sterile, and gray. The assessment room. The tall metal slab rose from the ground and Stathos-6 tossed Estrellas onto it. The lizard crawled over to a far wall and stroked it until a holographic screen in an alien language lit up. Stathos-6 plucked at a sequence of symbols until a loud hum vibrated Estreallas' body where he lay.

From the ceiling a pod slowly emerged from cold storage, a breath of fog clung to the outside of the tube as it came down. Inside… was Talia. Peacefully asleep within the liquid interior. Her long curly hair floated around her naked body like a dark blanket.

"What do you think, Stathos-1?" The lizard groaned. "Should we eliminate her mind? Hmm?" He hissed. "Er-aaassse her soul, empty the body?" Fast as a snap he slithered over to Talia and tap, tap, tapped on the glass-like shell. "I can be her for you. I can enter this body… is that what you want, Stathos-1? A human life with her? I can give you that. Just one more mind wipe and you won't know the difference."

Estrellas' inner turmoil worked on overdrive. He was screaming in his mind, unable to move anything except his eyes. He wanted to shout, 'don't touch her!'. His skin crawled and his belly rolled with nausea.

Stathos-6 crawled on all four lizard claws over to him and rose to a stand slowly. He dragged a talon down Estrellas' cheek and whispered in his throaty lizard voice. "We can be together this way, forever. I'll stay inside her until you love me, then we'll body hop for the rest of time." His breath stunk of rotten insects as he got even closer. "Fuck the mission. We'll just fuck each other."

Estrealls choked on his vomit, apparently his body could still throw up but he couldn't move. Stathos-6 finally noticed, rolled him to his side so the sick could fall, and spoke again. "Don't worry, it'll all be over soon."

Estrellas watched in terror as Stathos-6 walked to another wall and stroked it until a tray popped out with a pink goo filled syringe. Estrellas hollered on the inside, kicked and screamed in his mind, desperate to move.

Stathos-6 squirted a bit of the goo, clearing any air from the top of the syringe, and turned towards him.

The needle pricked the surface of his skin and just before it was plunged in, the lizard let out a hissing screech like a sick baby's cry.

Stathos-2's arms were wrapped around the lizard's head, her fingers rammed deep into its eye sockets. Stathos-6 wailed and flailed his scaly arms, clawing at Stathos-2. He raked through her clothes leaving behind deep red scratches that oozed blood, but still Stathos-2 held on. Pushing her fingers in deeper, two, three, to four at a time until nearly her whole hand was inside the lizard's brain. Neon blue and eggplant purple brain matter oozed from its eyes around Stathos-2's hands, until it collapsed with her on top of its back.

Relief would be an understatement for the feeling that flooded through Estrellas' body, if only he could move and jump, and pump his fists in the air. He could hear Stathos-2 breathing heavily from wherever she lay on the ground.

She popped up, wobbly, and smiling with Lizard insides splashed across her face. "Miss me lover boy?" She laughed. "Just like riding a bike!" She chuckled again at her own joke as she squeezed her sides and gasped for air. "I know you're laughing on the inside." She pointed at him and winked.

Hardly.

She patted his shoulder and went to the holographic display. She hummed to herself as she scrolled through. "Let's find you an anti-toxin, shall we? Speed up this process and get you out of that paralysis." She kept scrolling until she found what she was looking for. "Ah, here we are." She tapped a few symbols and another tray slid out from the wall. Inside was a large orange wafer, like an extra-large, flat thin cracker. Stathos-2 pulled it out and walked over to Estrellas. She opened his mouth, shoved it in, and held his mouth closed.

He could feel the wafer dissolving on his tongue, bitter, and bubbly. A tingling sensation slowly spread from the tips of his fingers and toes inward to his middle, until finally, he could move again.

He sat up, wiggled his jaw side to side and cracked his neck, sighing with relief. "Perfect timing, as always." He gave her a sly smile. "I wasn't sure if you still had it in you, after being sedentary for so long."

Stathos-2 dramatically bowed and laughed again. "My pleasure, *your highness*." She said mockingly as she flung her hair back and lifted her head like she was in a shampoo commercial while doing a little shimmy, like she hadn't just murdered someone. "And you obviously haven't met many politicians' wives, they're vicious." She said with a shiver before marching over to Talia's tube. "Let's get your girlfriend out of here, shall we?"

"Wait." He said as he swung his legs off the table. "There's something I need your help with first." He gestured up. "In cold storage."

"Stathos-1, it's freeezzing up here." Stathos-2 shivered and rubbed her arms. "What are we doing up here?"

"You wanted a new body, right?" He stated as if it was obvious.

"Ah, right, I just didn't realize that was a priority." She grumbled. "These humans aren't exactly built for the cold."

"I want to surprise Talia. *You* are giving her mom back, and *I'm* giving her Angela back, and *we* are picking out new bodies." He said with finality. "So, what's your type? Young, old, black, Asian?"

"Rich." She said, "I've gotten quite comfortable in the lifestyle."

Estrellas tapped a wall to bring up a display and scrolled through a list of human profiles. "Ah, here we are, tech mogul. Net worth, 40.2 mil."

"That'll do!" She glanced at Estrellas. "You should have told me what we were doing, I hid her mom's soul on the complete opposite end of the ship. You wait here and pick someone out for yourself. I'll be right back."

Estrellas nodded and continued to scroll profiles. Searching for someone within the right age range, and he was pretty sure Talia cared more about the person than their gender, but did have a slight sexual preference towards men, and no preference on ethnicity. He'd just have to fib a little bit about where the body came from. Maybe he could tell her that they were grown from scratch. Even though he was aware the cloning and growing thing never really worked out, they could never really hold a soul well, but she didn't need to know that. Besides, what was one tiny human life compared to the expanse of the universe, and their love?

Finally, he found a suitable male, he selected the profile and the hanging bodies, which were vacuum sealed, rotated like clothes in a dry cleaner. This human had golden brown skin, south Asian most likely, honey brown eyes, and shoulder length dark curly hair. He was muscular, but not overly so, and an artist. He was an orphan with no close friends, which would make life with Talia much easier. No baggage.

Estrellas tapped a few more symbols and the male's body swung over to a waiting tube. The clear doors opened and sucked the body in before closing tight. Liquid began filling and in no time the body would be ready for modification and inhabitation. Super strength, and rapid healing were standard, but Estrellas thought a few *extras* might come in handy.

Stathos-2 returned, out of breath. “Damn, I forgot how big this ship is.” She held up a small jar in triumph, that had a shimmering light shimmery gas like substance inside. “Got it!”

“Great! Your new body is ready, I’ll do you first.” Like it was just another day at the office.

Estrellas administered a sedative and began the process of removing Stathos-2. He secured her soul in a jar and brought Talia’s mom to a new tube where any modifications would be undone, then her soul reinserted.

When Stathos-2 awoke in her new body she repeated the process for Estrellas.

Easy peasy.

Chapter Twenty-Six

Epilogue

Talia

Talia twirled and danced in the small kitchen, listening to her favorite music while she flipped pancakes, wearing bike shorts and a loose t-shirt. Happy. She was so happy. She was living with the man that she loved, and in his new body he was an artist just like her, in their new home and talking about starting a family soon. She had her best friend back, her mom was acting like her mom again, and for some reason her dad had lost some of his bite.

She didn't remember anything after Bill's house. It was all an empty picture in her mind. But when she woke up, there was no longer any danger. She had her family, and Estrellas in a very attractive new body of his own, by her side. Peace was the only way to describe it. She was lucky and grateful and was not about to question that, not after everything she had just gone through.

She heard Estrellas before she felt him. His deep voice hummed along with the music as she felt his strong warm arms wrap around her waist.

He kissed her cheek. “Yum, smells good babe.” His deep sultry voice flooded her core with warmth.

“Your favorite, blueberry!” She smiled and turned in his arms so that she could plant a sensuous kiss on his full soft lips. As she pulled away, she saw the desire in his eyes.

He tugged her back into his arms and returned the kiss, deepening it. He rubbed a hand against her ass and pulled her tighter as his tongue searched for hers. She welcomed him. She slid a hand underneath his shirt and ran her fingers lightly up his toned back, feeling him shiver under her touch. He groaned against her mouth as their kiss gained intensity. She wrapped one leg around him to press against him tighter. He responded by clenching one hand more firmly on the roundness of her ass, and the other started to massage her breasts eliciting a gasp of delight.

Just as she started to reach down the front of his pants, a loud screech from the fire alarm broke the spell of their desire. Estrellas hurriedly reached for the pan where the pancakes were burning while Talia laughed. He dumped the pan in the sink and turned the water on, backing away quickly to block his face from the heat, then turned the burner off.

She covered her hand over her mouth and chuckled. "Well, there goes breakfast."

He turned the water off and returned her smile, and she stared into his perfect honey brown eyes, breathing him in. Pine and fresh scent lingered on his skin from his morning shower, his curls were still damp, and she lovingly tucked a strand behind his ear.

She saw an instant desire response in his body and heat flooded between her legs.

"Hmmm." He practically growled. "Who needs breakfast?" He scooped her up into his arms, with her laughing as he rushed her to the bedroom.

Estrellas

So what if they started their new life together on one little white lie? So, this body was stolen. That was a small price to pay. He was happy, she was happy, and that's all that mattered.

Stathos-2 had discovered that it wasn't true love, but a deep desire to belong to a specific place that severed the hive mind connection. Estrellas took comfort in knowing that his love for Talia was genuine even if his hive mind was still intact. But his connection faded the further the mothership got.

Stathos-1 and Stathos-2 had systematically gone through their brothers and sisters on the mothership, assigning those that wanted to stay on Earth a human body. So what if a few thousand human souls were displaced? His family was an endangered species and the humans had billions, it seemed harmless enough to him.

The rest of the Stathos's chose to move on and continue to explore the cosmos. The explorers eventually found a new planet to call home, planet Meraiis, and sent word to their brothers and sisters on Earth that they would settle there and no longer interfere with the affairs of others.

His kind would multiply, he was sure of it. He would take Talia's powerful last name when they married, and he knew Talia was pregnant before she did. They would name their daughter, Isabel Garcia, and raise her to follow in the political footsteps of her grandfather, The Speaker of the house. She would become the first female president someday; he was sure of it. She would be the fresh start Earth needed; she would begin the healing.

Sure, the alien offspring would be born with a few *extra abilities* and maybe it was selfish to live their own lives for their own pleasure rather than the greater good. After all, Earth was slowly dying, and their kind could probably save it. But why did that responsibility fall to his brothers and sisters?

That was the next generation's problem.

Stay Tuned...

The epic conclusion to the Stars Like Acid series, STARS RAIN DOWN, is coming March 18th 2025

About the Author

Marissa Lupe, Latina (she/her) of mixed heritage, has always found her safe place in the world of stories. Now, she's creating her own worlds in the scope of speculative fiction and hopes to provide the same joy to her readers.

Her first novel, *Stars Like Acid*, a sci-fi-dystopian mild romance was published September 18th 2023, and will be included in the Satisfiction book box in late 2024. Her second novel, *Stars Like Fire*, published on March 18th 2024. *The Bone Inventory* is her third novel, and her fourth novel, *Stars Rain Down*, the final book of the *Stars Like Acid* series will release March 18th 2025.

Beyond writing, Marissa enjoys anything artsy and creative, like making jewelry, painting, photography, and collecting crystals.

She currently lives in the Rocky Mountains of western Colorado with her family, connecting with the soul of the Earth through the appreciation of nature.